Golden Dominion

A Novel

by

D. S. Cuellar

Special Thanks to:

Editors:
Pauline Suite

Cover Art by Roslyn McFarland

This novel is dedicated to my father:

Frank Cuellar Jr.

Other Stories by D. S. Cuellar:

Guardian of the Red Butterfly

Guardian of the Monarch Moon

Guardian of the Shadow Warrior

Dead to Rights

A Mermaid Story

Golden Dominion

LOC # 1-13281147321

Visit us on Facebook at

Guardian of the Red Butterfly

GOLDEN DOMINION

CHAPTER 1

The late afternoon sun lit up the rainbow-colored stained glass that arched over the head of the Christ figure depicted in the window's mural. The beams of colored light came shining through the leaded glasswork and created a scene that was now filtered across the priest's bedroom. The terminally ill eighty-five-year-old monsignor barely had enough strength to raise his hand and point in the direction of the bookshelf across the room. With a slight French accent, he said, "There, on the middle shelf. The one about the history here in the valley."

A much younger hand of fifty years that belonged to Father Chance selected a dusty old book titled: History of the Napa Valley. Father Chance opened the book and after fanning the first few pages came to a carved-out section that held bits of old faded parchment within its hollowed-out square.

Father Chance carefully lifted out one of the frail pages, "What is this?"

"It is why you were brought here…" Before the elder priest could finish his sentence, he began coughing. It took him a moment to catch his breath and regain his composure.

Father Chance set the book on the bed and went to the window. He turned the latch and opened the window slightly to let in some fresh air. When he turned back, he saw that by moving the angle of the window, an array of colored light from the stained glass had moved slightly and was now cast upon the headboard just above the head of the monsignor.

Father Chance then reached out to him, "Are you alright? Can I get something to help you…"

"I'm afraid it's too late for that. God has other plans for me, as he has plans for you." The elder priest tried to reach out for the book but just did not have the energy.

Father Chance brushed his hand over the loose pages of the book that had folded back over the hidden pages. He removed more of the loose pieces of script within the cut-out portion of the book, "What is left of these bits of scripture isn't much."

"You are now entrusted with the Brother's secret that only a few of us have known, as you are now the guardian of the sanctity of this land."

Father Chance took a closer look at one of the pieces of paper. He saw what was left of some drawings of mechanical devices with passages from the Bible inscribed on them. The more he tried to separate the old, worn, and dry pages to look at them, they began to disintegrate and crumble through his fingers.

Father Chance watched as the dying priest used what strength he had left to reach up in the direction of the warmth coming through the window that was shining a light down upon him from the colorfully illustrated scene.

The monsignor asked Father Chance to hand him his set of rosary beads from the nearby nightstand. As he handed him the beads, he noticed where a cross should be connected below the last five rosary beads, was missing. Each of the five beads had a meaning. The first Our Father, followed by three Hail Marys, then the last one stood for another Our Father. He slipped the one-of-a-kind set of beads made from white pearls and black onyx into the monsignor's hand. The elder priest crossed his hands over his chest and began to pray, "Our Father who art in Heaven…"

"Monsignor, I am not the man you think I am."

"Yes, I've heard your confessions. I've learned over the years that we can either let our fears overwhelm us or we can use them to embolden us."

"Then you know, I am living a lie."

"What I know is this, you are no longer that man. I may be nearly blind in my latter years, but I've seen enough to know the physical scars we bear do not have to mark us with the burden of the evil men who gave them to us. Since I took you in, I've seen the man you truly are, and I saw it again when you took in those lost children and gave them a home."

The monsignor raised the rosary beads in Father Chance's direction. Father Chance leaned forward. The monsignor slipped the rosary over the younger priest's head. "These were given to me by Father Sebastian and now I am entrusting you with them. They are a part of this monastery and should never leave these grounds."

Father Chance sat upright. "I understand, Father."

"The Lord guided you on a path that brought you to this place in your life, now be the light to those who seek your help. Be that man."

The two men continued to pray together, "Our Father who art in Heaven, hallowed be thy name. Thy kingdom come..." And with the monsignor's last breath, they recited, "Thy will be done on Earth as it is Heaven."

With his right hand, Father Chance formed the sign of the cross over the now-deceased body of his friend and mentor. With his left, he closed the lifeless eyes of the departed.

Father Chance said a private prayer and as he did, he felt a draft come through the open window. When he opened his eyes, he stood to close the window but before he stepped away from the bed, he saw a few of the pieces of the frail parchment had lifted out of the book and were lying on the bed. One of the pieces caught his eye. He saw a partial date. He carefully took a closer look, and he could make out the numbers for August 13th, 19…

* * * * *

By candlelight, a steady 40-year-old hand, held a quill at rest. He dipped the end into the reservoir of black ink and then filled in the rest of the date that read 1923 onto the woodfree, uncoated page of a very well-used Bible. The monk carefully began to scribe a drawing over the scripture of the ancient text. When he was done, he removed the rosary beads he was wearing and laid them out on the table in front of him. He carefully removed the crucifix, picked up an etching tool, and moved the large candle he was working with a bit closer. He then went back a few pages in the bible to a page where he had written a few words, referenced them, and then began to etch them into the back of the cross.

The subterranean room of the monastery was dark with a bit of mist in the air. Dim embers glowed hot as the bellows breathed life into the firepit that was made out of flat stones. The youngest of the four monks, in his early thirties, held a set of tongs, and with a steady hand, reached in and took hold of a hand-forged iron melting pot. The tools being used were at least sixty years old, as liquified gold was poured into a hand-carved mold made from black walnut.

Another pair of hands reached in and took hold of a second mold that had been submerged in a basin of holy water to cool.

The mold was placed on the table in front of another monk. He opened the wooden mold to reveal an exquisitely designed silver medallion with an overall shape like that of a triangle.

A 33-year-old monk had a set of special skills that were handed down to him by his father who was one of the finest watchmakers and jewel setters within a hundred miles. The monk took a small file and began to smooth out the rough edges. The mold that had been filled with liquid gold was now carried by a set of steel tongs and set into a basin of holy water to finish cooling. Steam rose from out of the water creating a white mist that vaporized into the air.

A white linen cloth was laid out flat on a wooden table. A set of hands placed the gold medallion onto the white linen cloth next to the now-refined silver medallion.

The two medallions were identical in size and shape. They were designed with hooks and facets to become part of a whole.

Another monk who rounded out the foursome, also in his early 30's, began to polish a copper piece that had just been completed. He laid the finished product down on the table in line with the silver and gold medallions.

The copper piece was a masterful work of art and showed off four precious stones, perfectly set in place. A hand reached over to a set of the eight remaining precious stones. He carefully picked out a diamond and handed it over to the monk who was preparing to set another four stones in the silver section of the medallion.

There were 12 different stones in all and all of them an example of perfection. There was one stone to represent each of the twelve birthstones.

A set of hands added a couple of small weights to one side of a scale, then put a four-inch cylinder that was eight inches high onto the other side of the scale. The brass-plated cylinder was too heavy, so the monk unscrewed one end and poured out a bit of sand before setting the cylinder and the cover back on the scale. This time it balanced so the monk reattached the lid and lifted a counterweight from a set of scales. Then the cylinder was turned over and set on the table.

One of the four monks who was working in concert with one another stepped in and used a metal tool to add a punch mark in the center of the base. He then took the cylinder and attached the weight to the end of a chain on a grandfather clock that was positioned on one side of the small room.

When he lowered the weight and let the chain take the full amount of tension, the clock began to strike.

The stone setter paused and waited for the tones from the clock to die down before he continued to attempt to set the diamond in between the facets that were to hold the diamond in place on the silver medallion to see if it would fit correctly. Once he determined it was a perfect fit, he took a moment to hold the precious stone up to the flame of the candle next to him. He tilted the diamond from side to side, causing an array of various rainbow colors to shine across his face.

* * * * *

A rainbow arched high across the valley floor. Its familiar spectrum of colors stood out against the background of the grey sky. The end of the ark of the rainbow appeared to dissolve the closer it got to the Napa Valley Marina.

A seagull's flight skimmed just above the water on its approach as it flew inland toward the marina. The seagull banked, turned into the wind, flapped its wings, and slowed to a stop as it landed on top of a white 1900 BMW that was submerged in the river up to its roof. The car itself was just a few yards down the boat ramp from which it came.

The seagull let out a shrieking squall which caught everyone's attention. The bird's cry momentarily disrupted Hope from performing CPR on Michael, whose body lay, unconscious, on the wet pavement in front of her. Both Hope and Michael were soaked to the bone. Steam was rising from Hope's naturally wavy blonde hair and clothes. Hope, a real beauty at age 22, was not going to give up and continued with the CPR. Michael, whose pale skin and lifeless body showed no signs that he was going to make it to see his 26th birthday.

A small crowd had gathered, and the concerned voice of an older fisherman could be heard, "Is he going to be alright?"

Hope looked up at the fisherman and assured him with a look from her deep blue eyes, a look of faith that could only come from a deep and caring old soul, that Michael would be okay. She took another deep breath, leaned in, and gave lifesaving air to Michael. Michael began to breathe and cough up water. He flinched in pain throughout his body, especially his lungs. Although Michael was physically fit, with his whole body chilled to the bone, he still had to fight for air. Hope looked back toward the fisherman and gave him a reassuring nod.

All the fisherman could say was, “Thank, God.”

The once quiet and concerned crowd began to talk among themselves as they began to part, as the sirens that were once off in the distance had now arrived on the scene. An ambulance pulled up first followed by a fire truck. As the paramedics gathered their gear and the fire department controlled the crowd, Hope heard Michael trying to say something.

“I’m cold. I need...”

“You're going to be alright. Lie still.”

This was the coldest Michael had ever been in his life, “I can’t stop shaking.”

Two paramedics stepped in and attended to Michael. Hope stepped aside and began to talk with one of the firefighters.

The firefighter removed his coat and placed it around Hope's shoulders to help get her warm. Although most of the crowd had dispersed, there were a few who still lingered taking pictures and making recordings on their cell phones.

Just as Hope walked over to check on Michael's condition, one of the EMT's had just given Michael a shot to help sedate him to help his body relax from the shock his body was experiencing.

Just before the sedative was able to take effect, Michael looked up to the woman who just saved his life, "Who are you?"

Just before Michael blacked out, she replied, "Hope."

* * * * *

The Queen of the Valley hospital, a three-story medical facility, with its welcoming lush green shrubs and trees, had its familiar gold Queen Cross and Mary figure on its southern-facing tower had been around since 1958.

Everything about Michael's recovery room was quiet. The EKG machine was in silent mode and the oxygen he was taking in didn't make much sound other than when he exhaled into the plastic mask that covered his nose and mouth.

Adriana had her head down in prayer as she clutched Michael's hand. At age 24, she had the best of both worlds.

She had her mother's charm and good looks, as well as the same black hair and smooth olive skin that were both exotic and soft to the touch. She had her father's family pedigree and when it came to the family fortune, she was a rebel and was indifferent to it. As her mother and father used to say from the very beginning, she was trouble.

Adriana did not know if Michael could hear her as she spoke from her heart, "We are all praying for you, Michael. The whole family sends their love and best wishes to you."

Adriana let go of Michael's hand to use both of hers to wipe the tears from her face. She then reached back for his hand. It was not where she had let go of it. It had moved. She looked up for the first time to see Michael was trying to reach for her. Her large, beautiful, deep brown eyes were so happy to see he had awakened.

Michael had yet to gain his composure when he asked, "Hope, is that you?"

Before Adriana could reply, Michael's doctor entered the room right on cue after hearing Michael's question, "I think he might be referring to the woman who saved his life."

Adriana reached out her hand to greet the doctor, “Hello, my name is Adriana Bellacini. I'm Michael's fiancée.”

“Miss Bellacini, my name is Doctor Andrews. Michael is suffering from a concussion he received in the accident, as well as the effects of hypothermia. We don't know just yet to what degree. His vitals are good, and he slowly seems to be coming around. Try talking to him again.”

“Michael? It's Adriana, can you hear me? Can you tell me what happened?”

Michael began to come around, his vision faded in and out of focus, but his body was just not ready, and he slipped back into an unconscious state.

* * * * *

The night sky was full of stars. Only a few seemed to be hidden by the aura of the clear full moon. The reflection of the moon danced on the water of the marina as a boat passed at a low wake speed through the canal. The boat continued to slowly cruise past a row of sailboats that were all docked neatly side by side.

At the end of one of the peers, Michael sat on the edge of his 17-foot Catalina sailboat, as he saw a 43-foot Sun Odyssey sail past named the SEA GOAT.

With envy in his voice Michael muttered to himself, “Someday, I got to get me one of those.”

Michael sat alone at the stern of his boat, the Misty Wine. With only the ambient light coming from a down pool flood lamp high above on a telephone pole on the opposite dock, Michael could barely be seen. But he liked it that way. He was holding a small package that was wrapped in birthday paper. He unwrapped the gift and found himself holding a hardback book with no title. He opened it to the first blank page and saw there was an inscription along with a feather. He laid the feather in the crease of the opening page of the book then tilted it to get the best light he could to read the text that had been beautifully hand-written. That is when he recognized the handwriting. It read: Through faith, hope is a second chance. Happy birthday, Mom.

The night air brought a small breeze with it, and it lifted the feather from the book. Michael quickly snatched it out of the air, placed it back in the book, and then turned to the opening page of the story.

Chapter 2

The morning sky above the Napa Valley was crisp and blue with a touch of soft white clouds. An overnight storm had left the sky clear but there was still a sheer veil of fog hanging over the valley floor.

As the sun's warmth took effect, the fog began to lift, revealing ridges of the West side of the valley's rolling mountain tops. It made for a perfect backdrop for the monastery's exterior rough-edged design, stained glass windows, and red clay tiled roofs. The building was made from rocks that had been excavated over a hundred years ago from local gold and silver mines.

The monastery itself sat on a crown of land that overlooked the property. Most of the land was covered by vineyards in need of tending. Gravel roads ran East and West designating the property's northern and southern borders. A river, which was just on this side of its Western border, fed a large pond that was used to water one side of the property. The lower back forty had a reservoir that was fed from runoff, and a well that took care of the rest as needed.

As the sun's rays beat down on the handmade clay tiles of the monastery, traces of vapor rose from the roof as if a spirit was rising to heaven. A small cabin-like structure was attached to the North end of the building. Through a gap in the curtains of the living room window, a silhouette of a man was moving, then stopped.

Inside the structure, Father Chance was lying on the hardwood floor in pain, experiencing shortness of breath. Suddenly, from out of nowhere, a medallion landed on his chest. The medallion was about six inches in diameter. One-third of the medallion was made of gold with four precious inlaid stones. Another third was made of copper and another four stones. The other third was missing.

Father Chance put his hand over the two remaining pieces of the medallion that lay on his chest.

He spoke with sadness in his voice, "It appears I have failed you."

Father Chance was still in a slight daze and a bit of shock having been taken by surprise. He lay among pieces of a broken vase and shards of glass.

He knew his assailant hadn't meant to knock him over onto the antique coffee table but alas, there he was. His pain was more of a personal nature than physical.

Father Chance's heart was heavy, "Don't do this. You are only doing this because of greed."

The assailant who stood back in the shadows, slipped the third of the medallion that was made from silver into his coat pocket. The man was silent as he slowly began to walk backward, to leave Father Chance alone, lying on the floor.

The assailant's silhouette paused in the doorway and then he closed the heavy wooden doors to the monastery behind him, sending a deep vibration that Father Chance could feel through the floor. Father Chance, now in his mid-fifties, sat up and dusted himself off. When he tried to move, he felt a sharp pain in his left thigh. He rolled to the right and with his left hand felt a small piece of glass that was sticking out of his leg. He pinched it between his thumb and index finger, gave it a little wiggle to see if he could tell how deep was, and with a quick jerk pulled out the shard.

Father Chance heard the muffled sound of his cell phone ringing in his pants pocket from underneath his robe. He tossed the one-inch piece of glass aside and removed the cell phone from his pocket. He checked the caller ID. It read: Hope.

It wasn't long before Hope had made it to the monastery and joined Father Chance in the modest-sized kitchen. She took a seat at the four-person dining table that had one side pressed up against the wall. Father Chance had a breadboard with a chunk of cheddar cheese and a half stick of salami on it. “Hope, can you grab the bread and a sharp knife out of the drawer?”

Hope did as she was asked and while she was up also got two glasses of water, one for each of them. Once she was back at the table, she began to break off small pieces from the loaf of local sourdough bread. Father Chance had removed the crucifix from around his neck and was holding it in his hands as he pondered about what had just happened.

Hope paused from cutting slices of cheese to reach across the table and place her hands around Father Chance’s. Hope had listened to his version of what had just happened, but she knew there was something more that wasn't being said.

Hope asked, “What more can I do? I feel helpless.”

“You just being here is enough. What happened today was not your fault.”

Hope began to cut thin slices of dried salami from the stick of Molinari. “That's just it. You haven't told me who did this to you.”

Father Chance set down his rosery beads and then took Hope’s hands in a tender grasp.

“A lost soul has a way of finding the truth but cannot always accept it while seeing through the distractions to find the way home. That is where faith in God can make a difference.”

Hope put together a small plate for Father Chance and handed it to him. “You’re not going to tell me who did this, are you?”

“There is something I need to say to you that I’ve been meaning to tell you for the longest time.”

Father Chance pointed to the medallion on the table. He explained, “This medallion is the key to the survival of this monastery.” Hope picked up the medallion as he went on with his story, “I wanted to wait to tell you and Vincent together so that one day you both could take over this land and restore it to its former glory.”

Hope interrupted. She could see that Father Chance was tired and a bit confused about what had happened earlier. “Hush, Papa. When we’re done here, I want you to lie down and get some rest. We can talk about this later.”

“No, actually, I think we better talk about it now. You’re going to find out sooner or later. It might as well be now.”

Hope saw the deep concern in him and knew there was more he wanted to say. She held back from asking more of him than he was willing to divulge and began cutting a few more slices of salami.

Father Chance could no longer hold in the conflict that had been building up inside him. “It was your brother, Vincent.”

Hope was stunned. She dropped the knife she was using, and it rattled as it fell onto the ceramic plate. “Papa, why would he do this?”

“I told him about the history and the value of the medallion. How I had planned for you two to take over the land after I am gone. For whatever reason, he took a piece of the medallion and left. You must find Vincent. He doesn't know what he has done.”

*****

At age 24 Vincent Chance had a lot going ... what he didn't have was patience. He drove his car through the parking lot without a care in the world, and as he did, almost clipped a car that was trying to back out. His focus was getting into the empty parking space nearest the entrance of the restaurant. As he pulled his car into the parking space and came to a stop, his license plate not only reflected his family name but his lifestyle. It simply read: CHANCE.

The morning air was crisp, and Vincent's walk was too, as he made his way to the entrance of the River's Edge Restaurant.

The heavy entrance door closed and in the middle of it was a hand-painted carved logo of a trident with a bright orange crab stuck on one of its prongs. The name of the restaurant encircled the artwork with white cloud lettering and a midday blue sky background.

Inside the restaurant, Vincent made his way to the upstairs dining room. He was standing by one of the lightly tinted bay windows that had a view of the river on one side and the parking lot near the entrance on the other.

Vincent removed something from his pocket. He held the object up and placed it in front of the window so the sun's morning light could shine upon it. It was the silver third of the medallion. The piece itself had an arch just over six and a quarter inches and two sides that were each three inches in length. The sun's rays passed easily through two of the stones that were embedded in the piece, a diamond, and a red ruby. The other two stones were a dark solid piece of bloodstone and the other, a piece made from opal. As the beams of light showed through the diamond and ruby, they created two arcs of brilliant colors that crossed eight inches out from the silver section itself. Vincent moved the piece up and back, making the beam's focal points cross, and shine between his eyes just above his brow. A sense of euphoria came over him. Vincent lowered the medallion when he caught a glimpse of Michael's car as it entered the parking lot. He watched from above as Michael parked, got out, and started to walk away from his car. He was stopped in his tracks because the end of his trench coat had gotten caught in the driver's door.

Vincent was laughing to himself at the sight of Michael having a hard time fighting to free his coat. He watched Michael working the door handle to no avail.

Finally, the catch gave, and the car door opened. Michael freed the coat and made his way over to the restaurant.

Vincent held the medallion up to the window once more. As the sunlight passed through the precious stones in the medallion, the colors seemed to shine not only a brilliant array of color onto Vincent's face but also gave a sense of being seduced by a higher power.

Vincent began to believe this medallion was much more valuable than its stones and the silver crest that held them. “Amazing.”

Inside the restaurant’s first floor, Michael and Adriana were seated at the main bar. The bartender, Mario, put two coffees down in front of them.

Michael appreciated his good friend, “Thanks, Mario.”

Adriana felt the same way, “How's my Pisan doing these days?”

Mario being the consignment mixologist was always ready with a kind gesture. “Things are good. It's good to see you. A lot has happened since you've been gone. How was Italy?”

"Good. Had to go back and visit family and take care of some business."

"Two months is more than a visit."

"Learning the family secrets to help carry on the tradition."

At the other end of the bar, Hope set a case of wine on the counter catching Mario's attention, "Well, it's good to have you back." Mario gestured toward Michael. "This poor sap actually couldn't stop talking about you."

Mario walked away to tend to Hope. He did a quick count of the contents of the box, and it looked right. As he worked out the tab with Hope, Adriana thought Michael was looking Hope's direction a little too long.

Adriana turned to Michael and kissed him. "So, just how much did you miss me?"

"A little."

Adriana kissed him with a much deeper, passionate kiss.

Michael quickly gave in, "Okay, a lot."

"Did you miss me?"

"Of course. Although, I did get a lot more work done."

"I brought back a surprise for you."

"Let me guess. A bottle of your grandpa's 2018 Cabernet."

"Even better. Some of the vines."

"He gave you actual vines?"

"What he actually said was, they were an early wedding present for us. Something that will hopefully produce a new vintage that will stand out above all the rest. Those were his words, and you are family now, so you better not fail him."

Michael took a few more sips of his coffee. "I can't believe he gave us the vines. Maybe we can blend it with that 2017 you thought needed a little boldness to it because the smokiness of it was a little lacking." Michael took another sip of his coffee.

Adriana sipped on her coffee as she watched the wheels in Michael's mind turn in all directions with possibilities. "I told Nonno you would be excited."

Michael finished off his coffee. "Hey, do you want to go see the boat? I've finally got it to the point where someone can appreciate it."

"You can show it to me later. I'm more in a cozyin' type of mood. How about we go to the house? A nice warm fire sounds really good right about now."

"How did you get here? I didn't see your car when I pulled up."

Adriana rattled her keys in front of Michael. "I parked on the side. Do you think you can keep up?"

CHAPTER 3

Michael followed Adriana out of the restaurant and to her car. He didn't mind lagging a little behind; he enjoyed the view. She had one of those walks that caught a lot of attention. A nice pair of legs in a pair of faded jeans that always seemed to have a small rip just in the right place.

Michael slipped ahead and opened the car door for her. Adriana climbed in and started the engine of the 1980 Sports Mercedes 450SL. She always liked it when her father would let her talk him into taking it out for a spin. She had charm and her father always had a soft spot for her. Michael gestured and she rolled down the driver's side window.

"Follow me."

Adriana had a better idea. A fun idea. "No, you, can follow me."

Adriana put her car in gear and as she took off, the car fishtailed slightly. With the parking area still in the shadows of the cool morning air, the ground was slick. Michael watched as Adriana headed down the long drive that led her out of the marina.

Michael climbed into his car and unknowingly caught the end of his trench coat in the door jamb once again. He started his car and rolled down one of the back windows a few inches down to help circulate the air and defrost the inside of the windshield. He cranked up the controls on defrost settings and then started to back out into the lane.

Coming at him, he saw a large sailboat being backed in his direction heading for the boat ramp.

Michael put the car in reverse and began to back up to give the boat more room to maneuver. Instead of the car turning in the same direction as the wheel, Michael now found himself sliding down the boat ramp on the black ice that wasn't letting the tires grip enough to maneuver the car. A bit of fear crept in, and he cautiously hit the brakes. The car started to slide a little on a thin layer of ice that had built up on the boat ramp but after he spun the wheel in the other direction, he was able to stop the car from sliding back any further. Michael saw the back of the boat getting closer and figured the driver had no idea Michael was behind him. Michael tried to drive forward and work his way around the boat but found himself not going anywhere due to the ice.

Michael had good reason to worry. “This is not good.”

A man on a nearby sailboat saw what was about to happen and began waving his arms in a panic to get the attention of the driver backing the large boat but to no avail. “Stop! Stop!”

Michael saw the sailboat coming at him, but it was too late. Michael hit the horn just as the front of his car was struck by the back of the boat. Michael's head was thrust against the steering wheel. The sudden impact dazed him.

The car slid backward across the top of the frozen ramp, caught the main slope, and then descended frighteningly with ease into the water. The driver that was backing the sailboat stopped his heavy-duty truck and got out just in time to watch Michael's car lift from the surface of the road as it began to float on the water.

Another man who had just exited the restaurant heard the commotion looked over and saw Michael’s car now adrift. He turned back around, pulled the restaurant door open, and yelled inside to anyone within earshot, “I need some help over here!”

Michael, still dazed and a bit disoriented, tried to get the door open. The door would not budge. He caught a glance of the end of his coat caught in the door jam. The car began to sink.

As the cold water of the marina started to flow into Michael's window, the freezing water began to consume him. His fear of the water and the shortness of breath were evident on his face.

A seagull had been flying above the marina and was casting its shadow on the path in front of where Hope was walking toward her car. The movement caught her gaze, and she followed the path of the shadow across the ground which led her focus to look up and she saw a man in the distance waving his arms.

The man was frantically pointing in the direction of where the boat ramp met the surface of the water. “There is a man in trouble.” He cupped his hands around the edges of his mouth, “The car! The car! There is a man in the car!”

Hope looked over in the direction the man was pointing and saw the top of Michael's car even with the surface of the water. She began to run toward the water's edge.

Hope ran past Mario as he came out of the restaurant to check on all the commotion. She was filled with adrenaline as she shouted out to Mario, "It's Michael!"

Mario followed and when he was close enough, he saw air bubbles coming up as the car filled with water and was going under. Hope's thoughts had gone from a fear of losing her friend to having no fear at all as she ran across the grass. As she made her way closer to the water's edge, she threw off her jacket, paused long enough to kick off her shoes, and without hesitation, dove into the icy water.

Mario was already on the phone dialing 911.

Inside the car, Michael was twisting and turning trying to escape the confines of his jacket that was still pinned in the door. The freezing water was making it difficult for Michael to escape and he could feel the hypothermia starting to set in. Michael's body was now completely submerged. He could feel his body temperature was dropping fast. His legs had already started to go numb. As much as he wanted air, even if he could take a deep breath, his lungs were on fire and they felt constricted, causing his breathing to shallow. He was losing control of his senses as he felt stinging pain coming from everywhere.

His energy felt depleted and the last thing he saw before he passed out was Hope's face under the water at the driver’s side door.

Hope tried to open the door, but it wouldn’t budge. She saw the look in Michael’s eyes fade to nothingness. Then it hit her, she had much deeper feelings for her injured friend.

Hope felt her lungs fighting for air. She surfaced long enough to take a few deep breaths before holding the last one and she resubmerged. She tried the driver’s side door again, this time, it budged slightly. She put one foot on the side of the car and used the extra leverage to pull as hard as she could. The water had filled the inside of the car and an equilibrium had been reached, making it easier for Hope to open the door. As she did, the last of the air bubbles escaped the car and rose to the surface.

Hope tried to pull Michael’s limp body from his car, but he wasn’t moving. She resurfaced, took a breath, and saw Mario coming her way. She went under, reached across Michael’s lap, and undid his seatbelt. She felt Mario pulling from around her waist. As she came up, he went under and was able to pull his friend from the car.

As soon as Michael's body reached the surface, Hope took one arm and helped Mario to pull Michael from the frigid waters.

Together, they struggled to pull Michael's dead weight across the slick surface to the top of the ramp. They pulled off his long, heavy, watered-down coat, then laid him down on his back on the frozen pavement. Hope immediately began CPR. Others began putting dry jackets over Hope and Michael.

Mario told the man with the boat to pull it forward to make room for the ambulance that could be heard off in the distance.

* * * * *

Darkness. Fragments of disembodied voices off in the distance. Then a cool sensation, like a light breeze, but it was more direct. Then awareness, awareness he was alive. There was tension in his lungs from his body fighting to breathe. He felt fear in his heart like waking up from a bad dream. The thing was this was real. This feeling of pain was on the verge of more pain. Then there was that cool, wet sensation, again. Fever breaking and all five of his senses telling him that he had died but found himself waking up among the living.

Michael opened his eyes to see a nurse brushing a damp towel across his forehead wiping away the night sweats. She opened the small hand towel and wiped his face and all around his neck.

The nurse smiled, “Welcome back.”

Michael took a deep breath and out of reflex, he grabbed the nurse’s wrist. Michael tried to talk but realized he had a breathing tube taped to the side of his face and there were other tubes and lines carrying information to machines he could not see, but only hear.

The nurse reassured him, “You’ve made it through the hard part. Let me get your doctor.” She still felt the tension of Michael’s gasp. “You’re going to have to let go…” She felt the tension in his whole body relax and watched his head settle back onto his pillow. “You seem to be breathing okay so let me remove this airline for you.” She cautiously peeled back the adhesive tape and removed the line of oxygen from his airway. “Is that better?”

Michael took a hard swallow, “Yes. Thank you.”

The nurse took her leave and as she left the room, the door stayed open long enough for Michael to see Hope in the hallway just outside his room. He raised his hand as best he could as if trying to reach out to her. With no one around to stop her, she entered the room.

Michael's mind was still waking up and the puzzle he saw had a lot of pieces still missing. "How do I know you?"

The nurse reentered the room and answered, "She's the one who pulled you from your car and saved your life."

With each breath that Michael took, his focus became clearer, and he got a good look at the woman who was standing in front of him. The puzzle in his mind was slowly filling in. "It's you. I know you, don't I?"

The young woman reached out and took Michael's hand, "I'm Hope. We've known each other for a while. My family owns the vineyard next to yours."

Michael pulled his hand away and then tried to place both his hands on his head but all the tubes that were keeping him alive held him back. "What is all this?"

Nurse Chastain filled him in. "You've been through quite an ordeal. We've been bringing you back from a case of hypothermia. These lines have been taking your blood, slowly warming it up, then recirculating it back in."

"Why can't I remember what happened?"

The nurse saw that Michael hadn't taken his eyes off the girl and let her explain. "I overheard the doctor out in the hallway say you hit your head pretty good and that the frigid water had caused hypothermia, sending your body into shock. He said this might cause some loss of memory, but it should only be temporary."

"How well do we know each other?"

Hope smiled, "Well, our vineyards, Golden Dominion, butts up next to yours to the South. We've been neighbors for as long as I can remember." Hope took a moment to look into Michael's eyes to see if he was really in there or just messing with her. "Both our families have been in the business for a very long time. Although we may be rival vineyards, we seem to all get along."

"So, if you're Golden Dominion, who are we?"

"Ciel Bleu."

"Blue skies."

Michael and Hope looked at each other in a bit of amazement.

"You knew that?" Hope asked.

"I knew that."

"See, the doctor was right. You should be better in no time."

Hope could hear the doctor talking to someone out in the hallway. Michael reached out for her hand and before he could take it, she withdrew it and folded her arms.

"What's wrong?" Michael asked.

Before she could answer there was a knock at the door. A moment later, Adriana entered Michael's room and saw Hope standing at the foot of Michael's bed. "What are you doing here?"

"I was in the area and just wanted to check in and see how Michael was doing?" Hope turned to Michael. "I hope you feel better soon."

Adriana kept an eye on Hope as she left the room. She then added a smile to her face, turned to face Michael, and took his hand. "How are you feeling Michael?"

Michael once again leaned back onto his pillow and took a deep breath. “I'm still thirsty.”

Adriana reached over and grabbed a cup of semi-warm coco that already had a straw in it and helped Michael to get a sip. “I just spoke to your father. He is on his way and should be here soon.”

After wetting his throat, Michael saw the puzzle in his mind was no longer the same puzzle. “Who are you?”

CHAPTER 4

The sun's rays danced on the backs of the leaves from a light wind as they gave shade to the grapes maturing on the vine. Row after perfect row of ten years of meticulous labor had produced acres of an award-winning pinot noir for Bellacini Vineyards. Dark plump grapes dripping with dew clung in tight bunches along with swirling corkscrew-shaped tender vines of the late September fall-colored leaves.

The West side of the vineyard ended along Hwy 29 that runs North and South right up the middle of the Napa Valley. A paved road intersects the highway at the entrance to the property. The sign for the Bellacini Vineyard stood out as one of the more recognizable ones for the tourists who often stopped to take group photos in front of themselves before heading down the drive to the tasting room that was located just inside the gate.

There was a truck with its tailgate down standing next to a monitor. A two-man team seemed to be working in unison as one tweaked the controls on the monitor while the other man wore a set of First-Person Viewing goggles and had a remote-control device in his hand.

In the nearby field, workers were making their way up and down the rows pruning and prepping for the harvest as a drone flew high overhead.

A hand reached in and pulled a single grape from one of the bunches. The grape was squeezed and crushed between the man's fingertips. Robert Bellacini, a man in his early fifties, was a seasoned vintner who had done very well for himself and was already a pillar of the community. He crushed another grape and then lifted it close to his face to smell the aroma, then slipped the grape from its skin and put the sample to his mouth for a taste. He turned to Vincent who was a man about half his age. "What do you think?"

Vincent took a grape from the vine and went through the same procedure as Robert. "Very nice. Sweet, about ready."

Robert concurred, "Could be sweeter, maybe two more weeks."

Vincent pulled a rag from his pocket and the two men wiped their hands. They proceeded to walk between the rows to head back toward the main house.

Robert handed the rag back to Vincent, "Did you bring what I asked for?"

Using the rows of vines as cover, Vincent reached into his other pocket, pulled out another rag that was folded up, and handed it to Robert who carefully unwrapped the object. The bright sunlight glimmered off the four precious stones that were set within the triangle-shaped medallion made of silver.

Robert liked what he saw, "Did you have a hard time getting it?"

"No."

Robert's follow-up had a bit of grit in voice, "Then why didn't you bring me the entire medallion?"

"You said you wanted to test the silver content to see if it came from one of the Dominion mines. So, I got you the silver piece."

Robert's reply indicated the irritability he felt toward Vincent, "I asked for the medallion to test the silver. The… medallion."

Robert turned and walked away from Vincent, who then followed a few steps behind kicking up dust as Robert headed over to a nearby golf cart to take him back to the main house.

A low-flying drone that passed overhead caught Vincent's attention. He looked up and followed the drone's path as it flew off the Bellacini property and continued in a northbound direction as it gained elevation to navigate the skies over the Golden Dominion property.

*****

Robert drove up the main drive and when he reached the main house he was greeted by Bianca, who he had been with for nearly twenty-five years. The sun accented her beautiful Latino skin. Being six months pregnant at age forty-one highlighted her natural beauty. Her eyes were dark and had a sense of mystery to them and her long, black hair was soft and fluttered in a nice summer breeze. She looked up and saw the drone flying overhead. "We don't need to bring any more attention to this deal. Do you think another scan is necessary?

Above, the drone continued making passes from the Bellacini side and back into the airspace over the Golden Dominion vineyards. There was a device attached to the underbelly of the drone consisting of sonar capabilities and a camera. A red light was on indicating the device was functioning.

The drone made a wide arc and made another pass in the opposite direction as it gathered topographical details, as well as ground penetrating radar information that was sent back to the nearby receiver.

*****

Father Chance was on the front steps of the monastery watching the drone as it flew over the vineyard. After the drone passed, Father Chance walked down the path and rounded the right side of the monastery's North side of the church. Once there, he opened a small wrought iron gate that helped to partition off a section that held five gravestones.

There were four in a row that were all about the same modest size. One for each of the monks who had built the monastery back in 1923. What was different about these headstones was that there were no last names. First, there was Father Daniel, 1883-1947. Father Gregory, 1893-1970. Father Richard, 1898-1972. The last belonged to Father Sebastian 1890-1978.

Father Chance knelt next to the newest marker that was below and centered on the other four.

It read: Monsignor Timothy Murphy. 1935-2023.

Father Chance made the sign of the cross and said a silent prayer. After, he proceeded to speak to his mentor for the first time since his passing.

"I came to you a humbled and broken man. You still believed in me and took me under your wing even after you knew my transgressions." With a bit of anger in his voice, he asks, "I am a penitent man asking you to release me of the vow I promised."

He got a sense that someone was watching him. He looked around and saw no one. Still feeling a bit irrationally anxious, he took a second look. It was then he saw the pair of eyes that had been watching him. The eyes belonged to a doe. It ended up that she was not alone. She had two yearlings alongside her. The doe slowly turned and walked away followed by one of the little ones. It wasn't until he muttered, "Go on, catch up," that the small black-tailed deer skipped off.

Father Chance was reminded that he was there for more than himself. He stood and said one more silent prayer over the men who cared over this land their entire lives then headed back toward the front of the monastery with a new sense of self.

Father Chance entered the monastery. Once inside, he dipped three of his fingers into the basin of holy water and made a sign of the cross by touching his forehead with his finger, then he crossed his chest and finally brought his fingers to his lips. He looked to the ceiling graced with the painted image of an angel wrapped in a turquoise cloth. Her wings were majestically fanned open, and her hair was backlit by the rays of the sun that highlighted her natural beauty. This gave her a sense of grace announcing she was Heaven-sent.

Father Chance said a silent prayer to himself.

*****

The same image that was painted on the ceiling of the monastery had a replica painting hanging in the main lobby of the Queen of the Valley Hospital. A small sign next to the picture said it was donated by: The Brothers of the Golden Dominion Winery.

Nicolas Venturella was a man in his mid-40s, well dressed, and well-tanned. He walked past the picture in full stride on his way to the reception desk. The receptionist was just about to spit up her water as she was taking a sip when she saw Nicolas approach her.

“Are you okay?” Nicolas inquired.

The receptionist wiped her mouth and set down the bottle of water. She took a deep breath and gathered herself from being caught off guard at the sight of Nicolas’ well-defined and handsome features. To the receptionist, his tanned, olive skin made him look like he had just walked out of a GQ magazine.

“How may I help you, Sir?”

“My son, Michael Venturella, was brought in this morning. He was involved in an accident at the marina.”

The receptionist went to her keyboard and within a few keystrokes had the information on his son.

“He's on the third floor. You can use the elevator to your left.”

“Thank you.” Nicolas looked at the receptionist’s name tag, “Rebecca.”

Nicolas headed over to the elevator as Rebecca watched the rugged specimen of a man walk away. She took another sip of her water and made a slight fanning motion with her hand. Rebecca couldn't take her eyes off Nicolas until after he entered the elevator.

* * * * *

Adriana was on her phone texting as Nicolas and the doctor entered the room. There was a muffled cell phone ping coming from the pocket of Nicolas's designer jeans.

“I was just texting you to tell you Michael was awake."

Nicolas walked over to the side of Michael's bed.

“How are you feeling, Son? I was just talking to the doctor, and he says he wants to keep you overnight for observation. “Can you tell me what happened?”

Michael looked over at his father and gave him a concerned look in return. Adriana put her hand on Nicolas’s forearm. Nicolas looked back at her, and she nonchalantly removed it.

Adriana filled Nicolas in about the doctors’ previous concerns, “He may not recognize you."

Nicolas looked back at Michael, “Son, can you tell me what happened? Do you remember anything at all?”

Michael reached out and took his father's hand.

“It's okay Dad. I'm going to be OK. I know who you are."

The doctor placed his hand on Nicolas' shoulder to get his attention. “Just to be cautious, I would still like to keep him overnight. If he shows improvements and his numbers come back up to normal levels, we can probably discharge him tomorrow. We still have a few concerns regarding the effects of the hyperthermia his body experienced."

“Yes, of course.”

Adriana looked at Michael and then at his doctor.

“Why can't he even remember his own fiancé?”

“It's not about how much he loves you, but with which part of the brain he is using to store that memory. Different parts of the brain hold different bits of information. For instance, a love for a parent is in a different part of the brain than where he holds the feelings of a loved one or for a pet, or in your case, a personal relationship.”

Adriana leaned in and kissed Michael to give him plenty of time to sense how much she cared. As Adriana was kissing Michael, Nicolas turned away to give them their moment.

After the kiss, Adriana leaned back a bit and looked directly into Michael's eyes and asked, "Do you feel anything?"

Michael ran his fingertips across his mouth. "I felt the kiss and how much it must have meant to you, but it felt like…"

Adriana finished his thought, "A stranger?"

Michael was as confused as she was, "I'm sorry."

"I don't quite understand, but I understand."

Adriana turned and left the room.

Michael's doctor tried to give his patient some comfort.

"Give it some time Michael. Let this swelling come down and you should regain most, if not all, of your memory."

Nicolas was concerned. "Most of his memory?"

"In some cases, with head trauma and loss of memory, patients can sometimes lose small bits of information about a particular memory. It's like dropping a frame or two out of a film. You see and hear the picture but some of the specific details can get lost."

“What kind of details?” Michael replied.

“Let's not worry about that right now. Let's see what tomorrow brings, shall we?”

Before leaving, the doctor gave Michael a reassuring look then turned and shook Nicolas’s hand to also reassure him that he believed in time, everything should be okay.

Nicolas took a seat near the foot of Michael’s bed.

“The doctor said you were lucky that Hope was there to save you.”

“That's the strangest thing. I have some memories of her and not of Adriana.”

“Like the doctor said, a different part of the brain. You must have deeper feelings for Adriana.”

“What about you dad?” For a moment, Nicolas was caught off guard. “How well do you know Hope?"

“You know her better than I do.”

“She said we were neighbors.”

“She and her brother work the vineyard next to ours.”

“The one with the monastery?”

“Yes, the one with the monastery that is overseen by Father Chance.”

CHAPTER 5

The Golden Dominion Vineyards was one of the oldest vineyards in the Napa Valley and was known for having one of the best wines produced from this region, but over time it found itself in need of a lot of maintenance. The vines themselves were sturdy and in some cases were still able to produce enough grapes to make a small vintage, but once again, found themselves unable to produce enough to make a decent profit.

The Golden Dominion monastery stood over the same foundation as the one originally built in the 1920's that mysteriously caught fire and was burned to the ground in 1933. Upon rebuilding, the monks took three years before reopening to the public in the spring of 1936. With stone used from local quarries and rock that was excavated from mines. The foundation was as solid as a fortress, and the walls were almost two feet thick. It had a bell tower that, back in the day, was used to call parishioners to Sunday mass and ring out in celebration an announcement of christening or marriage. The bell has long been silenced since the building had not held a mass in many years. That was when Father Chance was brought in to manage the estate.

A car pulled into the heavy graveled parking area on the east side of the building. As Hope exited the car, she bent over and picked up some loose debris around the area and tossed it into a large 55-gallon barrel that sat in the corner of the lot before she made her way toward the main entrance of the monastery.

Inside the monastery, Father Chance sat in silence as he prayed. With the sun high in the sky, there was enough ambient light to project through the stained-glass windows showering multi-colored hues over the altar and beyond. The altar itself was made of what looked to be eight matching panels. Three on the front and back and one on each end. The base was made of stone from hand-chiseled four-by-six-inch rocks and mortared into place all around the outside of the base. The top was one solid piece of redwood slab from up the valley with a three-inch border with a hand-carved design of vines and grapes running around the entire overhanging rim.

The wall behind the altar contained three large stained-glass images. The one on the left side was of Saint Sebastian the patron Saint of Archers. The image depicted Saint Sebastian's hands and feet bound to a tree with an arrow protruding from his left thigh.

The center panel showed a scene depicting sunlight coming down from the heavens. At the right time of day, the sun would accent the orange and bright yellows in the center of the mural giving the effect of the burning bush on Mt. Sinai. The third panel on the right was of a dove representing the Holy Spirit. The dove's wings opened wide. Behind it, were rings of various shapes and multicolored glass with the brightest yellows working outward to the warmest of deep reds.

Just as Father Chance ended his prayers, the main doors to the monastery opened, filling the interior of the room with awe and enlightenment. As Hope entered, her silhouette was in contrast with the sunlight as she walked up behind Father Chance. She put her hand on his shoulder. He made the sign of the cross and pressed the strand of five beads of his rosary to his lips.

Father Chance stood and faced Hope, "How is your friend Michael?"

"I think he is going to be okay."

Father Chance took Hope's hand in his, "How about you? Are you going to be, okay? You took quite a risk yourself going in after him."

Hope gestured above the altar where a life-size figure of the son of God was hanging on the cross. The stained-glass windows behind the cross were slightly angled so the light from each of them pulled their focus to the center of the church where Father Chance and Hope were standing.

Hope smiled and continued, “I knew I was going to be okay. I had a higher power with me.”

Father Chance proudly responded, “And the boy you saved, had you.”

Hope may have saved his life but still felt a deep loss, “And what does he have if he doesn't have his memories?”

“Let us pray that his heart helps him find his way home."

Father Chance and Hope both turned and faced the altar. They close their eyes in prayer. After a moment, Hope lifted her head and turned to Father Chance.

“What did you mean when you said, you needed to tell me the truth about who I really am?”

*****

As the sun was setting over the Bellacini Vineyards, it was a daily reminder of the natural beauty that was the Napa Valley. A car drove up the main drive and entered the gravel-laden circular road that led up to the main house. The car stopped near the entrance of the tall white pillars that framed the home's entrance. The driver exited the car with a large envelope in his hand.

He looked up and saw Robert Bellacini on the balcony that overlooks the main entrance. The driver flashed the envelope and Robert gestured for the man to come in. As he made his way up the front steps he was greeted at the front door by a servant.

Robert was relaxing on the balcony enjoying a cigar when he was joined by the man delivering the envelope. The man waited patiently while Robert attempted to relight his cigar. Once he did, he reached out with his free hand and the man handed him the envelope. As Robert opened the envelope the man took a step back and waited for further instructions.

Robert slipped the contents of the envelope out onto the table. The images were of deep penetrating aerial photographs that were taken from the drone where the Golden Dominion Vineyards butted up against his property.

What stood out in the image were bright areas of red, orange, yellow, green, and blue. There were also black perforated lines indicating where one property ended and the other one started. There was a contrasting line that led from one edge of the Bellacini vineyards and ran through to the Golden Dominion property then forked off in two directions. One line ended close to where the monastery was located. Within the contrasted area between the two properties, there was a dark color change that indicated a blockage of some kind.

Once Robert understood what he was looking at, he dismissed the driver. "Thank you. That will be all."

Robert's daughter, Adriana, walked out onto the balcony and joined her father. As she did, she got a glimpse of the images that her father was attempting to slide back into the envelope without her knowledge of their content.

"Are those the images from the drone?"

"What do you know about them?"

"That same truck was here a couple of months ago. I saw it on my way in earlier. What do those colors mean?"

"I had some topographical images taken to check the content of the soil to see if we are where we want to be for the next season's harvest."

Adriana took a seat opposite her father and was about to ask him another question when he cut her off, "How was Italy?"

"The family is doing great. Nonno was happy to see me. He showed me how to do some grafting. Did you know Grandpa has a vine with three different varieties of grapes on it?"

"Your grandpa has been working on those vines for years. That entire row of vines as you walk out of his house must have twenty different mixed varieties."

Another one of the house servants walked out onto the balcony with a small serving cart. On the cart was a tray with various slices of cheese, salami, and crackers along with some French bread, and a small bowl of virgin olive oil, plus three small plates. The servant set the tray on the table as Robert and Adriana realigned their chairs. The servant then took three wine glasses from the cart and set one down by each plate. She then poured two of the glasses from a bottle of red wine. Once the wine was poured, the servant replaced the bottle and left without a word being said.

"Is Momma going to join us?"

"I think she's off doing her thing."

"You should be more appreciative of her doing her thing. She's keeping your workers coming back every year and keeping them loyal to us. Not only that, but she also has some of them working all over the valley for you collecting information on our competitors."

"What she's doing is, bringing in more and more of her undocumented family up from Mexico through work visas and the next thing you know…"

Adriana interrupted, "The next thing you know, you've got spies everywhere. Like I said, you should be more grateful."

Robert and Adriana began to partake in the evening's ritual of locally produced snacks and wine, Adriana, hoping to catch her father off guard and get an honest answer out of him, got in the first question.

"Can I ask you a question? I saw some papers on Nonno's desk about the monastery on the Golden Dominion property and their lease. Why would Nonno be interested in that?"

Robert took a little extra time savoring his wine to try to find justification for his response. “Your grandfather took over this vineyard when he was just twenty-five. Back then, he wanted to expand but found out the land the monastery was on had a 100-year lease. That lease is about to expire, and it has always been his desire to buy that piece of property.”

“Is that why Vincent was over here the other day?”

Robert took another sip of his wine rather than answer her question.

Adriana continued, “I've heard stories about the silver mines that run under this area. Is that what the aerial photographs were for?”

“It’s my understanding those mines dried up years ago.”

Adriana reached into her pocket and called his bluff. “Then why did you have him bring you this?” She placed the silver section of the medallion on the table between them.

CHAPTER 6

The interior of the monastery was quiet, but it had a rich sense of history within its walls. If one listened hard enough and took in its beauty, one could take in the story of its majesty. The natural light had faded and in the glow of a few well-placed candelabras, there was a pathway that led through what was left of the ten rows of pews on either side of the space. Off to one side of the altar was an adjoining hallway.

At the end of the hallway, there was light coming from a gap in a semi-closed door that led to a small room. The room was built as a storage room, but Father Chance had converted it to a bedroom for himself while he was tending to the monsignor. Even after his mentor's death, he was quite content to stay where he was for now. He removed his rosary beads, opened the top drawer of his dresser, and set them in a small box that had no lid.

In the other corner of the drawer was another open box with a set of dog tags. Above that box, tucked up under the lip of the top of the dresser, was a well-worn leather holster.

The nose of a 35mm Beretta could be seen peeking out from under a military-issued black wool hooded mask known as a Balaclava. He reached inside the wool mask and pulled out an old, weathered notebook.

Father Chance removed the full-length black cassock robe he was wearing and hung it up in his oak wardrobe closet. He then removed his button-down dress shirt and set it aside. He poured some fresh water into a basin that he used to wash with and freshen up before dinner. He relied on the moisture in the drying towel to get his back. He could feel where the towel brushed over the scars he carried from his past.

Out in the hallway, Hope emerged from the bathroom and was about to head back toward the kitchen when she looked the other way and caught a glimpse through the crack in the door of Father Chance in his room.

She could see there was a long scar across his back from where a bullet had grazed him across his entire torso which was the centerpiece of his dark history. There was also a circular patch of rough skin where a bullet entry had left its ugly signature. Other smaller scars were less significant and were less of a reminder of where he must have understood the meaning of "hell on earth."

Father Chance closed the top drawer and opened the next one down, where he pulled out a fresh black button-down shirt and slipped it on, as he did as part of his daily routine.

Hope quietly turned away and headed for the kitchen. She knew Father Chance had gone through something horrific in his past but knew better than to ask, hoping one day he would tell her when the time was right. That time never came.

From where Hope stood in the doorway to the kitchen, she looked back down the hall and saw Father Chance's silhouette fill the darkness as he exited his room. The closer he got as he walked out of the darkness and into the light, gave the illusion he was a ghost, then just as quickly, his silhouette turned back into a man of faith giving the impression he was forgiveness personified.

Hope had made her way inside the kitchen and was putting things on the table for dinner when Father Chance entered.

"Have a seat Father, I'll get the rest."

Father Chance took a seat at the table that was set for three. Hope placed a hot pan filled with ravioli and malfatti onto a hot pad in the center of the table. First, she served Father Chance and then herself.

She passed the fresh green salad to him, in exchange, he handed her the freshly baked French bread.

"Father, do you believe in ghosts?"

"If you mean we all have a past we'd like to forget, then yes." Father Chance had seen that look on her face that said she wanted to know more but was afraid to ask. He went on, "I've seen things and heard confessions that could only be attributed to war."

"Is that why you spend so much time up at the Vet's home?"

"I go there to spend time with people who just need someone to talk to who will not judge them for what they were asked to do for our country."

That was the most she ever got out of him on the subject and left it at that. She took the seat opposite him, and he began to pray over their meal.

"I said an extra prayer for you and your brother today."

Hope always liked hearing that but they both knew there was something else she wanted to hear.

He continued, “When I said I had something I needed to tell you, it has been a long time coming.” Taking a sip of wine, he quenched his thirst. “I don't have much to offer you and Vincent except for the simple life we have here.”

Hope stopped eating and gave him her full attention.

“All of this…” he went on to gesture with both hands aimlessly, “is all you kids know and I'm afraid it could all disappear sooner than we think.”

“You're scaring me, Father. Where are you going with all this?”

“I'm afraid we don't have enough money to buy out the lease when it runs out.”

“And when is that?”

Father Chance reached into a small basket that sat on the edge of the table that hugged up against the wall and was filled with the week’s mail. He pulled out an envelope, removed the letter from within and handed it to Hope who quickly scanned through the paperwork getting the gist of its contents.

“Father, this letter says the land could not be passed down to Vincent and me because we are not your actual heirs?”

“Before you say anything else, let me explain.”

Hope, filled with confusion, had tears in her eyes. She set the letter down on the table between them.

“It's true, I am not your actual paternal father, but that doesn't change how much I love you both.” Father Chance reached out and took Hope’s hand in his. “Your parents were working this land just as I took over as the caretaker for the monastery. When you were just three years old and Vincent was six, your parents disappeared. I knew they loved you both very much and would not have left you here unless they had a good reason. So, I took you in with the expectation that they would one day come back for you.”

“What happened to them? Why would they leave us here?”

"I don't know what happened to them and I did everything I could to search for them. God gave me more than a monastery to care for when he sent me here. He gave me the honor of looking out for you and your brother. I do not regret a single day."

"Does Vincent know?"

"No. I'm afraid he is dealing with enough demons as it is right now. At the time, he was old enough to remember them, but I think over the years he's accepted the idea I was his father."

"What were they like?"

"Your mother's name is Sofia. She was about, I think, around 24, maybe 25, when they disappeared. What I can remember of your mother, she was a hard worker and always had a grateful sense of self-being. You are a lot like her. You have her lovely smile."

"And my father?"

"Your father must have been around 28ish at the time, and his name was Diego. He was very charismatic. Everybody loved him. Whenever someone was in need, he was there. He was a good man."

There was a long silence between them.

Father Chance went on to surmise, "After ten years, the police stopped searching for them and presumed they were dead. Based on your mother's last entry, they even suspected foul play might have been involved."

Father Chance gave Hope the notebook that was her mother's diary.

"What's this?"

"After your mother and father did not return, I was going through their things, and I found your mother's diary. I almost forgot I had it until now."

Hope began to fan quickly through the pages. She found a picture of when Vincent was four years old, and she was just a baby. She flipped to the last page and saw the final entry. The only thing written on the page were the words, *I'm pregnant.*

Hope saw the date written in the corner. March 23rd. She looked at Father Chance who answered her question before she even asked it.

"Yes. That was the last day I saw your parents alive."

Hope went back to the previous page, looked at the bottom, and read aloud to Father Chance the previous entry. *I hope he doesn't find out.*

Hope looked up at Father Chance. "Is this what got her killed?"

*****

The rain had been coming down pretty hard for most of the day. The tiled roof shed the water into the drains that led to a downspout that guided the water into an old wine barrel. At the bottom of the barrel was a tap with a hose on it.

The hose ran for a few feet before disappearing alongside a set of pitched double doors that covered the entrance to the underground storage area. Inside an abandoned mineshaft, the hose ran to a tap attached to a sink that was part of a makeshift counter.

Diego, 32, turned off the tap and cleaned up all the prep mess he had made from getting dinner ready for his family. The space he called home for now was an abandoned mineshaft. The shaft itself had been dug out wider over time by Diego to accommodate his growing family.

Diego had cleared an area roughly equal to a double-wide mobile home. He had repurposed wine barrels and pallets for almost everything. Including the kitchen table where he placed the bowl of fresh salad next to the pan with red beans and rice. His two children sat patiently at the table.

"Vincent, did you wash your hands?" Diego asked.

"Yes, papa." Vincent waved his palms in his direction.

Before Diego could ask, Hope waved her hands, too.

Instead, Diego asked, "Hope. Do you know where your mama went? She said she would be right back."

"Yeah, but that was fifteen, twenty minutes ago."

Hope shrugged and waved her empty hands. Diego quickly grabbed a couple of flower tortillas from under the foil, added the red beans and rice followed by a little cheese, then rolled them into homemade burritos just the way his kids liked.

"You two, start eating. I'm going to check on your mama."

On his way out, Diego stopped near the double-door entrance and put on his faded Levi jacket and well-broken-in cowboy hat. He flipped a switch near the power cord that ran off the monastery above them. Two cords branched off into a different part of the space. One led further down, and when he flipped the switch, it turned on the lights in the back area where they slept on single mattresses laid across a double stack of pallets, for beds.

Diego stopped next to the wood stove before leaving and turned back to his kids. “Vincent, you watch your sister. I’ll be right back.”

*****

Diego emerged from the slanted double doors. He quickly closed them behind him to keep the rain from blowing in. His wife, Sofia, was nowhere in sight. When he passed the front of the monastery, he saw Father Chance working on a wooden shutter that had come loose in the storm.

“Excuse me, Father. Have you seen Sofia?”

“I think I saw her heading over to the main house a little bit ago.”

Diego waved, “Thank you.”

Diego was halfway to the house when he came across Bianca who was headed toward the monastery.

They both paused under a tree to get out from under the rain.

"You shouldn't be out in this weather, Senora Bellacini."

Bianca spat out a jab of sarcasm, "I guess congratulations are in order for you, too."

"What are you talking about?" Diego replied.

"I hear Sofia is pregnant." Diego had a blank look on his face. "I guess good news doesn't travel fast."

"I think Sofia would have told me if she was."

"I guess she would have if, she was sure." Bianca started walking away toward the monastery. "If she was sure it was yours."

Even in the rain, Bianca's words cut right through the air and into Diego's heart. Diego tried to gather himself but couldn't get over what or why she would say such a thing. All he could hear was the rain coming down all around him as he made his way toward the main house.

He remembered Sofia had been acting a little strange lately, could that be the reason why? He knew their love was strong and she would never want to be with another man. He stopped just short of the steps and could see a silhouette of Robert coming from his office on the second floor followed by another silhouette of a woman approaching Robert.

Diego watched as the two figures played out like shadow puppets. He saw Robert's hand raise then swing across and strike the woman. He could feel that slap in his gut and that fury made his blood boil.

*****

Sofia had one hand on the edge of the desk to brace herself and the other holding her face. Her hand on her face intensified the numbness she was feeling across her cheek.

Robert's words were as cold as his heart, "I told you, if you ever tried to blackmail me, you wouldn't get away with it."

Sofia looked up with tears in her eyes. "Diego knows nothing about what happened between us and never will. All I am asking for is better living arrangements for me and my family."

Robert looked over and saw Diego standing in the doorway of his office.

Sofia saw the blank look on Robert's face and turned to see what he was looking at. That was when she saw her husband, Diego. She saw the rage in his eyes and how they were locked in on Robert. "Mi Amore, it's not what you think. I was only here to ask for…"

"No, Sofia. Don't say another word." Sofia had never heard such painful words come from her husband before. "Leave now, Sofia."

Sofia began to slowly step backward but before she could take a second step, Robert reached out and grabbed her wrist. Robert gripped tightly, twisting, causing her body to turn at his will. When she had her back to Robert, he stepped in behind her and used her body like a shield.

"What are you going to do Mr. Salazar?" Diego took a step closer and then saw the pain in his wife's eyes and stopped. "Are you going to throw away everything we have given you for a little misunderstanding?"

"What you, have given us? We work for pennies on the dollar and live like rats while you live like a king!"

"Because I am the king around here. You will do as I ask and be thankful you have what I allow you to have."

"What king needs to hide behind a woman?"

Robert slowly let go of Sofia's wrist. She pulled herself away from Robert and cautiously walked over to her husband.

"Leave, Sofia. I need to have a talk with Senor Bellacini."

Sofia looked up into her husband's eyes which were still deadlocked on Robert. "Let's just go, Mi Amore."

Robert couldn't help but push the limits of what he thought he controlled. "Yes, Diego. Go. Go with our Sofia and raise…"

Diego pushed Sofia aside and lunged at Robert. The two men went hard at one another, throwing punches, and elbows, and causing pain upon one another however they could. The two alpha males traded advantages over and over until they ended up on the ground with Robert on top of Diego. Robert landed two hard punches to Diego's jaw and was about to land a third when he suddenly paused with his arm locked back.

Robert could feel the pain of where Sofia had stabbed him in the back of his shoulder with the gold-plated letter opener from off his desk. Robert got up off the floor and turned to Sofia. "You bitch!"

Robert felt even more pain when Diego pulled the letter opener out of his shoulder and then a second later felt it being driven deep into his lower right side. Robert dropped to his knees.

Diego reached out and Sofia took her husband's hand and together they headed for the door.

Robert reached back with his right hand and pulled the letter opener out of his back. He stood, and when he did, he slipped and caught his balance on the desk. Sofia turned and saw Robert lunging toward Diego.

Sofia jumped in between the two men. "No!"

In Robert's condition he did not have all of his faculties and his anger and pain kept his momentum going forward and the letter opener meant for Diego was thrust into Sofia's midsection. As her body fell to the ground, Robert was left standing there with the letter opener still in his hand and Sofia's blood dripping from it.

Diego was blinded with rage and adrenaline. He lunged for Robert, but Diego never felt the letter opener being thrust into his gut until it was too late. Robert just kept jabbing and jabbing until he saw the life drain from Diego's eyes. Robert let the lifeless remains he had manifested slowly fall to the floor. Diego's body landed near his beautiful Sofia.

Robert turned to make his way back to his desk. He made it to his seat and reached out for the glass of bourbon that had remained intact. He raised his glass as a toast to himself in victory and then finished the drink.

Sofia and Diego's bodies lay parallel next to each other. They were lying face to face when she slowly opened her eyes and saw the life she had with her husband was now only going to be a memory. She knew for the sake of her children she would have to play dead until help could arrive. She also knew help had better arrive soon and she felt she didn't have much time for herself and the child she was carrying. Her heart was telling her, that not only did she just lose her husband, but the life she no longer felt she carried from within.

*****

The rain continued its heavy downpour onto an empty 4 x 4 that had a small flatbed section on the back half. Rain was being funneled into the opening of an old shed that fronted an abandoned mineshaft and due to the slope that ran away from the reservoir, mud was creeping into the mine. Due to the loose footing, Robert could only go so far as to lay Sofia's body down next to Diego's.

As Robert went to leave, he was having a hard time getting his footing while he made his way up and out of the mine. Once he got outside, he rinsed off his boots in a small stream that had been created from the floodwaters that curled around the newly built reservoir, then flowed toward the entrance of the mine. Robert looked around and saw that when the reservoir was put in, it changed the configuration of the land, forming a small riverbed that led across the front entrance of the mine.

Robert followed the stream that led back toward the side of the reservoir that contained the overflow gate. He moved the 4 X4 out of the way then made his way over to the gate that held back the water and began to turn the metal wheel, raising the gate. Water began to flow from the reservoir, down the side of the hill, and when the water had built up enough, it ran into the mine.

Inside the mine, Sofia reached into Diego's front right pants pocket and removed his tarnished gold Zippo. After a couple of tries, she got it to light. She felt muck gathering up against her body as the rain continued to turn the floor into a flow of mud. She felt the large oak post she was leaning up against, move. She panned the light over to where the base of the post was in the ground, and the ground…was moving.

More water was now flowing into the mine and that's when she felt the post dislodge and fall away. When the post collapsed, it fell across her legs, pinning her in place.

Sofia screamed in pain as the weight of the beam had just broken her leg. She dropped the lighter into the mud extinguishing the flame. In pure darkness, she reached for her leg and grabbed where the beam had left a gash in her thigh. She felt the warmth of her blood as it slowly pulsated the life from her body.

Even through the pouring rain, Robert could hear Sofia's scream funnel out of the mine. He started to go to the entrance but realized it was too late. The water he had released was now rushing past him and down into the mine.

Robert found himself sitting in the rain in the front seat of the 4 X 4 having lost all track of time. It wasn't until he heard the sound of the water pump from a nearby well kick on and started to refill the reservoir, once the water reached a minimum level. The sound of the motor snapped him out of his self-imposed misery. He made his way back over to the overflow valve on the side of the levee and cranked the valve closed. He thought to himself, between the well and the rain, it wouldn't take long to cover up his misdeeds

Robert turned to go back to the 4x4 and was stopped in his tracks when he saw Bianca standing next to the vehicle.

That was when Robert pledged to Bianca, that he believed the bodies would never be found, and that if she kept quiet, he would help with getting the rest of her family from Mexico and give her an interest in Bellacini Vineyards.

Without saying a word, one way or the other, Bianca turned and began to walk on her own, back to the main house.

*****

Hope looked up to Father Chance, "I guess we'll never really know what happened."

CHAPTER 7

The surface of the water contained in the large rectangular reservoir was calm, so calm, there was an almost perfect reflection of the full moon including what was known as a moonbow. There was a circular optical illusion of all the colors of the rainbow that surrounded the heavenly body.

The stillness of the water began to change as a series of small air bubbles started to break through the water's surface, which were followed by even larger bubbles escaping from an air pocket.

Beyond the confines of the reservoir, off in the distance, the Bellacini family home could be seen sitting up on the highest point of the land.

In the late hour, from the front of the house, most of the lights on the first floor could be seen going out, followed by a set of lights coming on in the large corner room that faced the front of the house.

Inside Robert’s lavish office, Robert took a seat behind his desk and pulled the chain on one of the lamps that sat on either side of his calendar desk pad, then the other. Vincent took a seat in one of the two leather chairs that sat opposite the desk.

Robert opened the top right-side drawer, removed the silver piece of the medallion, and placed it centered on his desk.

“What we need is more evidence to validate the mine’s content and we can't do that until we obtain the rights to Golden Dominion.”

“I haven't found any mine entrances on our land other than the one in the wine cellar of the monastery.”

“What are you talking about?”

“Father Chance once said, Dominion’s wine cellar is an expanded mineshaft, and I've been down there many times. As far as nonferrous materials go, it's dry.”

“Have you checked? Have you gone as far back into it as you can.

“No. There is a solid wall of wine racks right before where the floor begins to decline.”

“I want you to go into the cellar and see how far back the mine goes. Look here.” Robert showed Vincent a part of the scan of the topical map the drone had created. He pointed to where the monastery was located. “There appears to be two separate mines, running parallel, that travel for a great distance on each side of the monastery.” Robert pointed to one to the North. “It’s hard to tell, but this one seems to have collapsed beneath the monastery. Either that or all the rock in the building is interfering in the drone scan.” He then pointed to the one on the South side that runs under the left edge of the building. “This one here is where the wine cellar is and you can see, here, this shows the shaft goes on quite a ways before coming to this blockage, here.” Robert pointed to a dark section in the path of the tunnel. “How soon can you get back in there?”

“If I can find a way in, I can do it tonight,” Vincent replied, eager to please, hoping if he could find something, he would get part of the claim.

“If you see anything at all that looks to be made of a ferrous material, I want you to bring me a sample of it right away.”

“Of course.”

Robert picked up the silver piece of the medallion and held it up between him and one of the lights on his desk to get a better look at it with its splendid craftsmanship. "If the medallion came from this region, we have to assume the rest of the metals came from nearby as well." Robert reached back into the desk drawer and pulled out a two-inch cubed plastic case. It contained a gold nugget roughly one inch in size that was shaped like an asteroid weighing 28 grams and was worth approximately $3000. I've had both this nugget and this medallion recently tested, and the results say they have similar impurities that are found in this region of the valley. We're close."

"Let me do some research…"

Robert cut him off. "No! I don't want any of this getting out until we know for sure, that land is ours." Robert had a glint in his eye that reflected the gold nugget he was holding. "I'm having a hard enough time trying to control Adriana. I've asked her to do one thing and she's taken it way too far."

"How did Adriana know about this?"

"Thanks to you running your mouth, she does now. You piqued her interest."

“To her, it's just a silver medallion with some fancy stones in it. She doesn't know its true value.”

“She went through my desk, and not only did she find the medallion, but she also found the ICP spectrometry analysis.”

Vincent sat forward in his seat. “What did you tell her?”

“I didn't have to tell her anything. She read the God damn report! She saw that the concentration of the impurities matched this area, specifically, the Old Dominion mine.”

“So, the silver came from here, what's the big deal? The silver in all those old mines has long been excavated.”

“So, where did the gold come from? Who made the medallion and more importantly, why?”

*****

Vincent entered through the front doors of the monastery as quietly as he could. As he closed the door behind him, it became very dim inside, but he could see a light coming from down the hallway beyond the altar. He figured Father Chance was up late reading at the kitchen table as he often did.

Vincent made his way down to the center of the church. When he reached the pulpit area, he turned left at the altar, entered the hallway, and stopped in front of a door on the left that led down into the cellar.

Father Chance was not in the kitchen; he was on the opposite side of the altar. He had just come out of the other hall that linked to the storage area when he saw Vincent stop and enter the door to the cellar.

Vincent flipped the switch for the lights. There wasn't a lot of lighting but enough to get around in the space. He pulled a flashlight out of a drawer from a cabinet Father Chance kept near the bottom of the steps.

Vincent made his way to the back side of the cellar to the wall that was eighteen feet across and eight feet high that held different varieties of Dominion's Chardonnay wines. He checked both ends of the wall and found the right side had a gap that was wide enough for him to slip in behind the rack and gain access to the rest of the shaft.

Father Chance was at the bottom of the steps and could see light whipping around from behind the rack as Vincent made his way down into the abandoned portion of the mineshaft.

Vincent slowly made his way deeper into the mine. The shaft averaged about seven feet high and eight feet across. The deeper he went; he could see where the shaft would splinter off to the left and then abruptly end. He figured they must have been searching for more of the vein but came up dry.

The air was getting heavier the deeper he went, and the temperature was dropping. Up ahead he saw the floor shimmer. He stopped and picked up a loose rock. He tossed it as far as he could into the mine. He heard the splash of water and decided to turn back. As he made his way out, he took a second look at the walls and the loose impediments on the ground for any sign of silver or gold. Nothing. After a few more steps, he paused when he felt something oddly shaped under his shoe. He stepped back and found the object with his flashlight. It was a small green plastic Army man.

When Vincent had worked himself around the end of the rack and back into the main portion of the cellar, he saw Father Chance leaning against the old wood stove near the steps that led up to the slanted doors, giving access to the cellar on the side of the foundation. "Why didn't you tell me?"

"Tell you what, that you were born and raised in this wine cellar until you were six years old? Granted, it wasn't a cellar back then. You had enough trauma in your early years, there was no need to stir all that back up again. I was hoping your parents would return and that would be that. When they didn't, I fulfilled my promise to them."

"And what was that?"

"If anything should happen to them, I would take you and your sister in, and raise you as my own."

"And why did you?"

"Because, if I had gone through the proper channels, there was a chance you and your sister Hope would have been deported back to Culiacan. Your parents came from Mexico to give you a chance at a better life. I was just keeping my promise."

Vincent looked around the cellar and saw the wood stove Father Chance was leaning on and the memories of his father cooking there when he was a child, came rushing back to him. "I hate this place."

Vincent turned and threw the toy soldier back over the wine rack and deeper into the tunnel from which it came. He then headed for the stairs.

“Vincent.” Father Chance’s tone was calm.

Vincent stopped.

“Vincent, anger is not something you can replace, it is something you need to let go. A good person produces good things from the treasury of a good heart, and the evil person produces evil things from the despair of an evil heart.”

“Father, I don’t need a bible quote. What I need is money, money, that I don’t have. They threatened Hope if I didn’t come up with the money soon.”

“Oh, Vincent…”

“Father…” Vincent couldn’t finish his thought. He took one more look around, put back the flashlight, then left.

Father Chance heard Vincent slam the door at the top of the stairs. He then made the sign of the cross and started to pray.

CHAPTER 8

A set of train tracks ran parallel between Hwy. 29 and the Ciel Blue Vineyards. About this time every day, the Napa Valley Wine Train with its 1950's engines and 1917 Pullman Dining Car was headed up the valley toward St. Helena. It passed right in front of the gates that led onto the Ciel Bleu property. After the train passed the entrance, the black wrought iron gate on the right that led onto the property swung open. A maroon GMC Sierra 1500 Denali Ultimate crossed the tracks and headed down the long drive that was lined with a variety of colors of hybrid rose bushes. It made its way down the lane toward the house as if passing through a rainbow of elegant, sweet fragrances.

As the gate closed, the right and the left sides of the gate matched back up and proudly displayed the logo for the Ciel Blue Vineyards. To the left of the gates was a four-foot-high post stylized with red brick with a mailbox on top. Across the side of it read: Venturella.

The Denali made its way around the circle drive and pulled up to a stop near the main entrance of the home. Nicolas exited the truck and started to come around to help Michael, but he had already exited the vehicle on his own.

"I'm okay Dad. I may have lost part of my memory, but I haven't forgotten how to walk."

"The doctor said you might be lightheaded for a couple of days."

"No more than usual, right?"

Nicolas walked alongside his son as they made their way up the red brick steps, onto the landing, and then into the house.

Once inside the home, Michael was greeted by his mother, Jillian. Michael made his way over to one of the recliners and took a seat.

Jillian couldn't have been more motherly as she grabbed a homemade Afghan she had crocheted herself, and covered Michael's legs with it. "I called Adriana to tell her you were on the way home. She should be here any minute."

Michael raised his feet in the recliner, and no sooner had he closed his eyes to get some welcomed rest than there was a quick knock at the door followed by Adriana letting herself in.

Adriana walked up to Jillian and the two ladies greeted each other with a quick hug. "How's he doing?"

"Okay but seems a little out of it. Maybe it's the meds the doctor gave him?"

Adriana took a seat next to Michael, and as she did, took his hand in hers. "Your dad let me know you were getting parts of your memory back. I guess that's a good sign." She could tell by Michael's lackluster response he was still not quite himself. "Do you know who I am?"

"Yes, you're Adriana. We met yesterday."

There was a hush in the room as everyone took a cursory pause followed by a smile in jest from Michael.

Adriana continued but wasn't one hundred percent in her conviction. "I was worried there for a moment that we would have to fall in love all over again."

Jillian gestured to Nicolas and they both left the room for Adriana and Michael to have some time to themselves.

Michael took a breath. “About that.” His words caused Adriana to purely focus on Michael as he continued, “Yes, I know who you are, and that I have some feelings for you, but I don't think what I am feeling, is love. It comes across more like a friendship. Like two friends who grew up together but…”

Michael's father, Nicolas, was in the entry between the living room and the kitchen. He was taking in their conversation.

“But what Michael?”

“Something's not right.”

Adriana had a sense and looked back over her shoulder and saw Nicolas, who then turned and quietly headed for the kitchen. She turned back to Michael and took a moment to find the right words, “Here's what I know is right. Us. We are good together.” Followed by another deep breath, “Our families have been planning for us to take over the family businesses one day and combine our properties, along with Dominion. In doing so, we will have one of the largest and best-loved series of wines in the valley.”

“What are you talking about? What does the Dominion have to do with us?”

“On my trip to Italy to see my grandparents, I saw the plans for our families to buy out the Golden Dominion’s lease when it ends.”

“And what about Father Chance and the monastery?”

“Michael, we have a chance to become one of the best-known vintners in the Napa Valley. We can either tear it down or turn the monastery into a private tasting room for all three properties. Who cares? One day it will all be ours.”

Michael got an uneasy feeling from deep inside. He released the footrest on the recliner, got to his feet, and headed for the front door. As he placed his hand on the inside handle, he paused, then slowly turned the handle, and opened the door.

When Michael walked out onto the front porch, he took in a deep breath of fresh air as he felt the warmth of the sun on his face. The main road that led to the house wasn't that far from the property line of the Golden Dominion Vineyards. He didn't have to look too far away to see the monastery that sat on top of a small knoll about a half mile away. Adriana stepped out from behind Michael and joined him on the porch.

Michael was resolute, “There's no way that building is coming down. That monastery has been around for a hundred years or more, and we should be looking to register it as a historical landmark, not tear it down.”

“Fine. A tasting room then.”

Michael looked at Adriana with disgust on his face. He felt angered and betrayed for some reason, that he couldn’t fully explain. He raised his right hand as he walked off the porch indicating he just wanted to be alone and started to walk in the direction of the Dominion property.

“Where are you going? You should be resting.”

*****

There was a single row of vines that ran along the main road leading to the highway. It stretched the entire length and acted as a soft barrier between the two vineyards. A small three-foot rock wall ran parallel to the single row of vines that indicated the true property line. Beyond that, was another single row of vines that belonged to Golden Dominion to the South.

As Michael created some distance from the house, he could see Hope on the Dominion side walking his way on the road that ran parallel to their side. As Michael and Hope closed the distance, he could see she had a small bunch of grapes in her hand. Michael reached out and removed a small bunch of grapes from one of the vines on his side.

Michael slipped through the row of vines. Hope followed suit and met him at the rock wall. They took a seat on the wall, side by side, facing opposite directions. Michael felt something between them that he did not sense he had with Adriana, more of a kinship. “My dad always said, your vines are one of the best in the valley, and in the past, you had one of the best Cabernet Sauvignons and Pinot Noirs in the region.”

“Is that your way of telling me you want a tour of our wine cellar?”

*****

Inside the Golden Dominion’s wine cellar, there were rows and rows of dusty racks that filled the cavernous space. With no natural light to help illuminate the space, Hope had to use a flashlight to help navigate the dimly lit cellar.

Hope reached out and removed a bottle of Pinot Noir from the middle of one of the six-foot-high racks. "Here's a 2015 that turned out nice. It was the last year we had a full-time bottling staff, roughly, sixty-five cases that year."

Michael reached out gesturing for the flashlight and Hope handed it to him. He began to pan the light over the racks, scanning through what was left in the selection. He then pulled one of the bottles. "So, besides the Cab and Pinot, it looks like you have a Chardonnay."

"Father Chance always said, focus on making a few great wines rather than trying to appeal to everyone and overworking the land."

"Have you ever tried the Heitz Cellar's 1961…"

Hope cut him off. "Martha's Vineyard Cabernet Sauvignon." She paused. "No. Have you?"

"My dad took me to an event a few years back and someone had won a bottle for making a donation, a very large donation I might add, at a fundraiser for the Napa Valley Film Festival…"

Hope cut him off again. "I'm so jealous. How was it?"

"If the valley sun had a flavor…a light mint morning with a black cherry afternoon and light oak sunset."

Hope threw her shoulder into Michael's. "You're killing me."

"Personally, I think Dominion could rank right up there as one of the best if you could get back online. You were close once. You could do it again. You've got the grapes. You just have to get back your vision and find the right people with the right passion."

Hope saw something in Michael that was holding him back. Faith. She had known Michael a long time and always thought he could be as good a vintner as his father but never truly believed in himself. She remembered he always used to talk about wanting to see the world but instead, followed his father's dream for him to take over one day. She didn't realize how much she would miss him as a friend when he went off to UC Davis to get his degree in Viticulture. As soon as he returned full-time and began working for his father, the next she knew was, he was engaged to Adriana.

Michael looked around the wine cellar making a few hand gestures from side to side. "So, it looks like you have three wines at roughly 65 cases each. That's about a full acre per producing vintage, meaning you have about 9 to 12 acres of vines producing a very small sample and the rest is going to waste."

"According to what I found out last night, we won't have too much longer to worry about that."

"The lease?"

"Yes." Michael and Hope exchanged what they each had left of their handful of grapes to one another. "How did you know about the lease?"

"It sounds like once the lease is up, my father and the Bellacinis have a plan to buy out Golden Dominion for Adriana and me to take it over."

"Is that what you want?"

"Not at all."

Michael and Hope were surprised to hear Father Chance's voice come from somewhere over by the entrance of the wine cellar, "That's good to hear."

Hope looked over in his direction, “How long have you been standing there, Father?”

“Long enough.” Long enough for him to see the way Hope looked at Michael but he wasn’t going to tell her that. He took a few steps in their direction and gestured about the space. “Are you two up for a history lesson?”

Father Chance reached out and Michael handed him the flashlight. Michael and Hope followed his lead as he headed toward the back wall of the cellar. Once there, he pointed the flashlight’s beam through the back of the rack.

There was a void behind the rack and the flashlight’s beam faded into the darkness.

Father Chance handed the flashlight back to Michael and stood back. Michael and Hope moved in closer for a better look. They both scanned the area beyond the wine rack and saw the same thing. Nothing. Well actually, it wasn't nothing, they saw a tunnel that ran far beyond the illumination of the flashlight.

After getting a good look, Michael and Hope joined Father Chance closer to the middle of the cellar.

Father Chance elaborated, "This cellar…" Michael used the flashlight to pan around and get a better look at the entire space they were standing in. "… is an abandoned mineshaft. You see, there are no natural caves in the Napa Valley. Vineyards have to have them built into the sides of mountains or in some cases, below the winery. What you get is a constant temperature of between fifty-five and sixty-five degrees for storing the wines."

"Tell me more about the lease Father. Is there anything we can do to take it over after it runs out?"

Father Chance looked at the two of them, "Come with me."

Father Chance grabbed a bottle of red and then headed back toward the steps that led up through the set of angled exterior doors that ascended to the parking area on the South side of the monastery.

CHAPTER 9

Father Chance, Hope, and Michael made their way around from the side entrance of the cellar to the front porch. They sat back in their wooden rocking chairs in the shade created by the overhang.

Father Chance began to reminisce, “This valley has been good to me but I'm afraid there's not much we can do about the lease. We don't have enough product or viable vines to use as collateral to get enough money to buy out the lease once it comes up.”

Hope was heartbroken. “How much time do we have?”

“A couple of months maybe.”

Father Chance opened the bottle of Pinot Noir and poured each of them a taste using old jelly jars as glasses.

Michael couldn't imagine this land without the monastery. “Does the monastery have first right of refusal on the property once the lease is up?”

"Yes, I believe so. As I said, we don't have the assets it will take to show we can back the loan to make the offer."

From the porch, Michael took a good look around and saw the potential the land had to offer. Off in the distance, over at the Bellacini vineyards, he could see fieldworkers pruning the vines.

*****

Workers were making quick work as they pruned the rows of vines preparing for the upcoming harvest. A flatbed truck with wooden crates was slowly moving down the aisles as workers trimmed the vines of unwanted leaves and debris. Some of them tossed the debris into the smaller wooden boxes and others tossed the debris into the larger crates on the flatbed.

The day was already warm, and the workers took a water break from the coolers on the back of the flatbed when it would stop every fifty feet or so to load debris.

Robert, as head of the Bellacini family, enjoyed taking walks through the vineyard during each stage of the process. For as long as he could remember, this was his life, and he loved every aspect of it.

Alejandro, the head foreman, paused his work when he saw Robert making his way closer to him. “Hola, Senior.”

“Hello, Alejandro. How is the work coming along?”

“Everything is on schedule, Sir.”

“That’s good to hear. I'd like you to take the backhoe to the back forty. Looks like someone shot a deer last night down by the creek and left it there to die.”

“Sure thing, Boss.”

Robert started to walk away then paused and turned his attention back to Alejandro. “Make sure you bury it deep and add some lye.” Robert didn't wait for a response and continued toward the main house.

*****

Robert sat comfortably behind his desk drinking a freshly brewed iced tea enjoying the slight breeze from the slow whirling ceiling fan. He sat down his glass of tea and picked up the small clear box that contained the gold nugget. He knew there had to be more. A lot more.

On his computer screen were spreadsheets that showed his business assets. On the split screen was a pending offer to buy the Golden Dominion vineyards for $1.5 million, along with some assets coming from Ciel Bleu Vineyards.

Adriana entered the room; Robert set down the nugget, clicked the mouse and closed the screens. Adriana took a seat across from her father. They both knew she had an agenda, and it was only a matter of time before seeing who would blink first.

Adriana made the first move. “Tell me the truth about Dominion.”

“What do you mean?”

Adriana picked up the small plexiglass box and shook the nugget around like she was about to roll a set of dice on a Las Vegas craps table. “I think I deserve to know, don't you? There's more to that vineyard than the vintage isn't there?”

“That there, what your holding, according to my data, shows there's a lot more from where that came from.”

“That's why you had the aerial photography done. To find the locations of the old mineshafts.”

Adriana set the encased box back on her father's desk. "So, the real reason to buy Dominion isn't for its yield, it's for the land it's on." Robert could see the wheels in Adriana's mind slowly turning. "Does Nicolas know?"

Robert hesitated to give an answer. Adriana took this as a sign it might take a little coaxing. She put her feet up on the edge of the desk. She flaunted her sensuality as her tight TWIN PEAKS t-shirt showed off her braless, small but nicely rounded breasts. Her skirt was made from an old pair of jeans that normally hung about mid-thigh but when she placed her feet up on the desk it allowed the skirt to expose just a little bit more.

Robert couldn't help but notice that Adriana had an ankle tattoo of two small fish in the shape of a Yin and Yang design. "That's new."

"Yes, it is. Do you like it?"

Robert took the double entendre as a question, *"Do you like what you see?"* Robert's eyes followed Adriana's legs to the curve of her butt cheek that was exposed on the edge of the chair under her skirt.

Adriana played her hand. "What? It's not like you haven't seen my ass before. I left my iPhone on as you asked."

Adriana drew back her foot and rested the bottom of it on the edge of the desk, and in doing so, lifted her knee to expose just a little bit more. “I know you've been watching us.”

“You just play your part, and you'll get more than enough to cover your efforts.”

“Is that what you call having your own daughter sleep with your business partner? An effort?” Adriana slipped her feet off the edge of the desk and walked over to the door. With her back still to Robert, she paused before leaving and played her final card just to irritate him. “I think I love him.” Adriana left without another word being spoken by either of them.

Robert moved the mouse and woke up the screens of his computer. He passed the cursor over a file designated: A&N. He opened it and a half dozen video files appeared. He clicked on the third one and the video file started playing. The sound was so low, he couldn’t really hear it, but it didn’t matter. He was more interested in the content.

There, on the screen, was Nicolas on his back with a young naked woman straddling him. She was grinding over him and he was caressing her breasts. The woman threw her head back and Robert could finally see the woman’s tantalizing face.

It was Adriana. Her body started to quiver. Nicolas sat up and held Adriana in his arms. She wrapped her legs around his waist then after her release, she fell back onto the bed, her body glistening from her conviction. Just before the clip ended, Adriana turned and looked directly at the camera on her iPhone knowing, unbeknownst to Nicolas, someone besides herself would be watching this recording as well.

*****

On the Bellacini vineyards, there was a large water reservoir about the size of an Olympic size pool. Along with natural rainwater that was fed into the reservoir, its water level was maintained from a nearby well. It had wide solid berms on all sides that were flat. On top of the man-made structure was a three-foot path that encircled the water storage area.

There was a small breeze that formed a slight ripple effect across the water that distorted the reflection of the clouds that had started to roll in.

Vincent was walking around the far side of the reservoir scouting the land based on one of the land maps he had with him. Across the top of the plan, it read: Bellacini Vineyards Land Deed 1939.

He looked around to make sure he had his bearings correct before rolling up the map and then tucked it under his arm. Unfurling a second map that was labeled: Golden Dominion 1935. After deciding he had the right location, he held the two maps up, side by side, and the two topographic maps showed a series of mineshafts that ran under both properties.

Vincent walked up the incline of the outer edge of the berm that made up the outside of the reservoir to get a better perspective. He looked at the map once again and saw what looked like one of the shafts had once had an entrance near his current location. On the map with a designation mark: GDG-4.

To Vincent, there was nothing even close to looking like an entrance other than an old, dilapidated shack about the size of an outhouse. He rolled up the maps and stuck them inside his backpack.

As Vincent got closer to the shack, he realized it was a little bigger than he first thought. It was about five feet wide and ran about ten feet in the direction of the downside of a mound it was on. He pulled some downed branches out of the way and found what looked like a latch that, over the years, had rusted through.

He gave it a good kick and dislodged the bracket. It took a bit of work to clear the ground around the base of the door but once he did, he was able to pull the door open.

Vincent had to take a step back from the rancid smell that had built up from inside the tunnel. He turned his face into the wind to help clear his eyes from the pungent quaff that told him there had to be a dead animal in there. The odor had traveled up his nose and into his mouth forcing him to try to spit out the taste of decay that had invaded his mouth. Once he collected himself, and most of the vapors had cleared, he was able to take a better look. At first, he thought it might have been an air shaft but once he got a better look, he realized it had once been a working tunnel that was about four feet wide and six feet tall.

After he was able to get most of his senses back to somewhat normal, he took out a marker and circled the location on his map indicating the tunnel entrance.

CHAPTER 10

Nicolas drove the Dodge Ram 2500 work pickup down the same heavily graveled road that led to the main house where Michael had stopped to talk to Hope earlier in the day. Inside the truck on the passenger seat, there was a set of rolled-up surveyor maps being tossed around.

Nicolas reached out and held on to the maps as he slowed the truck to a stop, trying to keep them from rolling off the seat and onto the floor. He had stopped the truck to check the grapes on the vines because, at a glance, he thought they might be ready to harvest sooner rather than later.

Nicolas plucked a few grapes from one of his vines and crushed the grapes in his fingers then tasted them for their content. He thought they tasted fine and felt as long as they continued to get the same full days of sunshine that they had been getting, the harvest was only days away.

Nicolas looked just beyond the rock dividing wall that separated his vineyard, Ceil Bleu, from Golden Dominion and took a good look at a row of unkempt vines on the Dominion side.

At first, he thought, what a shame it was to see it all go to waste, but then thought, he didn't even know if any of it was any good. He slipped under the row of vines on his side, climbed over the short wall, and pulled a few grapes from the Dominion side. He did the same thing as before, crushing a few grapes between his fingers, then tasted them for their content. He was surprised and taken in by the flavor. He crossed over the side road and made his way into the main body of what should be this year's harvest. He tossed the few grapes he had in his hand, knelt, and grabbed a handful of the soil. After breaking up the soil in his hand, he then put a sample of the dirt on his tongue.

"What do you think?"

Nicolas spit out the soil sample and turned to see Michael standing a couple of rows away. Michael walked around the end of the row and met up with his father.

"You tell me."

Michael knelt, grabbed a handful of earth, and crushed it in his hand before giving it a taste. “The pH level in the soil is as good as ours, the whole vineyard needs pruning, and the grapes have a nice deep color. Soft yet plump. What more could you ask for? Speaking of asking, what's the asking price for Dominion?” Before Nicolas could answer Michael continued, “You know, once the lease is up?”

“This is strictly business, Son. We're buying this for you and Adriana. Can you imagine what this vineyard can produce?”

“I don't have to imagine, Dad. I just had one of the best Pinot Noirs I've ever tasted.”

“The 2015, I'll bet.” Nicolas turned and headed back toward the truck. Michael wasn't satisfied and had more to say so he followed his father. At the truck, Nicolas could see on Michael's face that he was still looking for an answer.

Nicolas gestured toward the truck, “Get in.”

Once inside the truck, Nicolas collected the maps that were on the passenger seat and tossed them onto one of the back seats just as Michael opened the passenger door to get in.

Nicolas got the truck headed down the road and took a fork off to the left heading away from the house. After a short drive, he slowed and drove along a ridge that overlooked the Dominion side.

Nicolas stuck his hand out the window and followed the contour of the land. "Every time it rains that slight slope keeps the vineyard from being flooded and ruining the grapes. I believe the real gem is what's on the other side of that slope, the side that faces West. Some of the best grapes in the region are on that land and I want you to have them. That's the sun side, the more sugar side, and I'll bet that's where that fifteen Pinot came from."

"Dad, can I ask you something?" Nicolas turned his attention to his son. "Why did the Bellacini's come to you for this deal?"

"Son, this deal…is for your future. Why wouldn't I be interested?"

"Then why haven't you asked me what I thought about the deal?"

"The deal is going through one way or another, that's why."

"What does he have on you?"

"Why would you ask me that?"

"You once told me not to invest your own assets in such a merger because if it fails whoever has possession can control the outcome. Mom showed me the deal. We are out of position. If it doesn't go through, it invites the Bellacini's to take control of our land to cover the loss."

"There isn't going to be a loss! Trust me."

"That land belongs to the monastery and Father Chance. Why can't we help him restore the land instead of buying it out from underneath him? We can then blend our reds with theirs and get one hell of a vintage out of it."

Nicolas quickly stopped the truck causing the tires to lock up on the dusty road. He shut down the engine and got out of the truck. Michael saw the frustration on his father's face, but he still had to press him for an answer, so he got out of the truck and joined Nicolas on the side that overlooked Dominion.

Nicolas wiped his brow. "Son, I know you are friends with them over there, but we have an opportunity to expand for pennies on the dollar, and Son, that is how business is done. Don't you get it? I'm doing this for your and Adriana's future."

"Dad, these are your plans, not mine."

“What are you talking about?”

“One thing that is becoming clear as I get my memory back is, I don't have the same feelings for Adriana, that she has for me.” Michael gestured with his hand out in the direction of Dominion, “If you're doing this for me and Adriana, don’t.”

Michael didn't wait for a response from his father and got back into the truck.

Nicolas took a deep breath and got back in behind the wheel. “All I've ever wanted was to give you a head start like my father gave me. There’s a lot more going on than you know.”

“Don't get me wrong, Dad. I appreciate what you're trying to do. But I don't want to take over Dominion at the expense of Father Chance.”

Nicolas started the truck back up, found a place to turn around, and headed back toward the house. “I want you to understand something, Michael. This buyout is happening. We have investors and banks already working on this. It's not personal.”

"It was personal when you said you were doing it for me. What's changed?" When Nicolas didn't answer and instead, changed his focus toward the road, Michael turned to see Hope walking up a path on the Dominion side. "You can let me out here."

Nicolas stopped the truck long enough for Michael to get out before heading up the road toward the main house. Michael worked his way over to where he found a low place in the wall and crossed over it to meet up with Hope.

It came across to Hope that Michael's conversation with his father did not go over very well. "How are you feeling? Are you okay?"

"I will be. I want to get a better look at what Dominion has to offer." Michael continued in Hope's stride back in the direction of the monastery. "Is there any more of that Pinot left?"

*****

Back inside the monastery, Michael and Hope had been waiting by the altar and were rejoined by Father Chance who was walking their way with an armful of maps and land deeds.

Michael helped Father Chance unburden his load by taking a few of the survey maps and spreading them out on top of the flat surface of the altar. “There's got to be something here we can use to hold off the sale of the land.”

“Did you learn anything from your father?” Hope asked.

“I found out that it's not about me and my future. I got the feeling there’s more to this deal than he’s letting on.” Michael flipped through a few of the maps, and they all seemed to be various versions of the same thing. “There has to be something more here that we are just not seeing.”

Father Chance paused. “I think what we are looking for may not be in these maps. I saw a drone flying over from the Bellacini side to ours in a grid pattern. Why would they be scanning and taking pictures when there’s plenty of information already available?”

Michael and Hope began trading pages with one another, and in doing so, Michael tipped over his glass and before he could stand the glass back upright, he spilled a little of the wine onto the floor.

When the wine hit the ground, it made a small clean spot on the floor that no one had noticed. It revealed a piece of bright blue colored tile that had a bit of white in the center of it.

Hope and Father Chance were focused on a notation on one of the old property maps that indicated where one of the original mineshafts had run under the property, and where it almost intersected with another shaft. In between, was a small circle with three evenly split sections.

Hope put her fingertip over one-third of the symbol. “What does that look like to you?”

Michael moved in a little closer to see what she was pointing at. “What did you find?”

Father Chance reached inside his shirt and pulled out the medallion he had hanging around his neck. He lifted it over his head and laid it on the page next to the symbol. “It may not be anything. It just may be coincidental.”

Michael just needed something tangible. “At this point, I'll take coincidental.” This was the first time Michael had seen these two portions of the necklace that were linked together. One was made of gold, and the other, copper.

He picked up the pieces and noticed that each contained four distinctive stones. "This is amazing." He turned it around and held the pieces up toward the open front door to use the light to get a better look. "What kind of stones are these?"

Father Chance took the copper piece from Michael. "Let's see. This piece has a pearl, a purple amethyst, the yellow one is a topaz, and this last one is a blue sapphire."

Michael held out the gold piece. "Looks like this one has a piece of emerald and turquoise. I'm not sure of the other two."

Father Chance pointed to the other two stones. "That one there is a red garnet and the black one is a piece of sardonyx. It was given to me when I took over as curator for this monastery."

"What happened to the missing piece?" Michael asked.

Hope answered with a bit of disappointment in her voice. "It was recently stolen."

"Do you know by whom?" Michael asked.

Hope looked to Father Chance with disappointment in her eyes.

Father Chance let Michael in on what had been burdening him. "Vincent has it. Before you say anything, he must have had a good reason for taking it."

Michael needed clarity. "What reason could there be for him to betray you like that?"

Father Chance moved a few paces toward the benches and took a seat in the pew in the front row. "He did ask to borrow it, but I refused."

Michael was still holding the two remaining pieces of the medallion. "By the weight of this, this section must be pure gold and the other piece looks to me to be made of copper. Every one of these stones seems to be different. What is the missing piece made of?"

"Silver." Father Chance replied. "All three of those elements were mined in this area, that much I know."

"These stones must have some value. Maybe we can get it evaluated and we can present the medallion to the bank as collateral."

"That medallion is a part of this place and never will leave this monastery." Father Chance replied matter of factly.

Hope moved over and sat down next to him. “Father, Vincent took that piece for a reason. I'm going to try to find out what that reason was.”

Father Chance knew the reason was money but didn’t want Hope to think any less of her brother than she already did, so for now, he kept it to himself.

Hope turned toward Michael. “I need to go into town. I could use your company. I want to find out just how much time we have and how much collateral we actually need.”

Hope didn't wait for an answer and started walking toward the door.

Father Chance looked up at Michael, “It looks like you're headed into town.”

CHAPTER 11

Hope's car pulled into the parking lot of the assessor's office that was located in downtown Napa. Michael exited the car after Hope and needed to pick up his pace if he was going to catch up with her as she made a beeline for the main entrance.

Once inside the assessor's office, Hope made her way up to the counter with Michael right on her heels. She looked down and saw the nameplate that read: Myra Robles, assistant to the assessor. After Myra logged in a few things on her computer, she gave her full attention to Hope.

"How may I help you?"

"We'd like to talk to someone about when our lease will be up and how much collateral we will need to take over the property when it ends."

Myra made a few clicks on her computer and found the correct search engine. "Can I have the address of the property or the name of the business please?"

"It's the Golden Dominion Winery," Hope replied.

There was a gentleman who was sitting behind the clerk a few yards away who perked up when he heard the request for information. He quickly stood up and walked up behind Myra. Myra took the cue from her boss and stepped aside.

The man took a quick look at the computer screen and then turned his attention to Hope. "Hello, my name is Andrew Marchetti. I am the assessor assigned to the Golden Dominion case. How can I help you?"

"My name is Hope and this is Michael Venturella. My father's fellowship has run the Golden Dominion vineyards for the last one hundred years. We understand the lease is coming up soon. We would like to know how much time is left on the lease and the amount of collateral we will need to retain the property."

"The monastery's lease on the property runs concurrent with the lease of the land itself. Both leases will end in about ninety days."

Hope turned to Michael with a bit of excitement in her voice, "Okay, we have ninety days."

Andrew looked at the monitor and confirmed the dates in question, “Actually, offers can be taken as of ninety days out and no later than thirty days before the end of the lease. So, as of today, there are sixty days remaining to make an offer.”

Michael got as close as he could to the counter to get a peek at the monitor, but from his angle, he could not see the information well enough from his position. “Okay, what about collateral? Can we use the property’s assets to cover the buyout?”

The assessor did not hesitate to respond since he had been working very closely with both Robert Bellacini and Nicolas Venturella on the possible takeover. “I'm afraid that property hasn't shown a profit in over fifteen years. However, because the monastery is the current lien holder, the monastery would have the first opportunity to buy out the lease. If the monastery cannot come up with the assets, we will then start to prioritize the offers.”

Michael counters, “How much will you need in assets?”

"In this case, based on the current value and the condition of the property, we would need the whole amount in cash to buy out the lease. I'm sorry I couldn't have been of more assistance, but I must be going, I'm late for a meeting."

The assessor closed the page on the monitor and then excused himself. As he walked by his desk, he picked up a briefcase and headed toward the side exit leading to the parking lot.

Hope turned to Michael with desperation, "He said the full amount. How much is that?"

The assistant clerk, who felt she had been slighted by her boss, walked up to the counter, and slipped Hope a small piece of paper. Hope took the paper looked at it and then shared it with Michael. The note read: 1.5 million.

*****

On the way home, once again, Hope was driving, and Michael was in the passenger seat as they headed North on Hwy. 29 making their way up through the valley.

"Michael, how much do you think the inventory in the cellar, along with the machinery, and the vines are worth?"

"You'd be playing right into their hands. Selling off the assets would lower the value of the property and in turn lower the amount of collateral needed. That would make it easier for them to come up with what they would need to take over the property."

"Not to sell them, to go to a bank and show them as assets."

"I get what you're saying, but unless you can show more value than the amount of the loan to keep operating after you buy out the lease, the bank is not going to take the risk of having to wait for you to make a payment or default." Michael took a moment and then reflected. "I know I have a stake in Ciel Blue that I got when I turned eighteen. Maybe I can sell it back to my father."

"I can't let you do that, Michael."

"Why not?"

"That is for your future," Hope replied. "I can't ask you to give away what your family has given their heart and soul to for three generations."

"So, where does that leave us?"

Hope and Michael headed on up the valley in silence for a while. They passed the Mustard's Grill on their way through toward Yountville. Aptly named for the surrounding area and nearby vineyards which are abundant with a sea of bright yellow mustard flowers indicating warm weather is coming as a sign that spring is on the way.

"I thought you said you wanted to stop by the grill for a bite to eat?"

"Lost my appetite at the assessor's office."

"Do you mind if we stop by the Olive Oil Company? My mom was talking about needing a few things from there plus we can get a snack at the shack."

"I love that place. You get the salami and I'll get the smoked cheddar."

*****

Inside the Olive Oil Company, Michael and Hope were making their way around the quaint Italian grocery store. Hope paid for her few items and then waited for Michael to finish his shopping. Michael walked out with a cardboard box filled with more than he had planned on as it usually was with the local hidden gem. He set the box down, pulled the salami from the box, and took out a pocketknife.

"Is that thing clean?" Hope asked.

"Clean enough."

Michael sliced enough for the two of them before Hope took the knife and sliced through the smoked cheddar. They each picked up a slice of each and toasted one another then dove into their afternoon snack.

"So simple. So good." Michael boasted.

"This smoked cheddar is the best."

Hope put her head back to take in the warmth of the sun on her face and took a deep breath. Michael couldn't help but appreciate and take in her natural beauty. The way the sun highlighted her shoulder-length dirty blonde hair and soft skin. He watched her smile as she took in the moment.

"What are you thinking about?" Michael asked.

"Isaiah."

"Who's Isaiah?"

"I will remain quiet and will look on from my dwelling place, like shimmering heat in the sunshine, like a cloud of dew in the heat of the harvest. It's from the book of Isaiah."

Hope opened her eyes and looked at Michael. “How is your faith, Michael? Do you believe in miracles?”

“I guess so. Why?”

“Because looks like we're going to need a miracle after all if we’re going to help Father Chance save Golden Dominion.”

CHAPTER 12

Vincent slipped inside Robert Bellacini's toolshed and started rummaging through cardboard boxes marked: painting gear. He found what he was looking for, a full-faced respirator. He began looking around the shed for what else he might be able to use. It wasn't long before he found an old miner's pickaxe. He added the tool to the small backpack he slung over his shoulder.

Just when he was about to leave, he took a second look at the old footlocker the pickaxe had been sitting on. He slipped it out from under the lower shelf of the workbench and dusted it off. He flipped open both latches and when he opened the lid, he saw a series of rolled-up maps.

The first one he unrolled was an old topographical and geological map of the land the Golden Dominion winery was on. It had a section of the land sliced away, like a whole three-layered cake cut in half, showing the topsoil then rock with quartz mixed in followed by another layer of a clay mix then more dirt.

Cross-cutting through the layer of quartz was a mineshaft. The shaft ran for over two hundred feet before splitting off into two separate shafts running parallel for another three hundred feet. In the corner of the map next to the reference scale was the date: 1892.

Vincent turned the page to see a copy of the same map dated 1908. In the second map, just beyond where one shaft had forked away from the other, it showed a collapse. He thought about it for a moment then remembered the quake of 1906 that hit the Bay Area. He figured there must have been enough of a jolt from the initial shockwave and subsequent aftershocks to collapse one of the tunnels.

When Vincent checked the next map, he saw that it was a more recent map of both the Golden Dominion and Bellacini properties. Most of the map was done professionally but part of it had some added lines that were hand-drawn, showing the location of the monastery on the Dominion side and the large reservoir on the Bellacini side. Next to the reservoir, was an X inside of a small box.

*****

The blue skies over the Bellacini vineyards were sparsely laden with white clouds that were being blown in from the Bay Area. As the afternoon breeze faded, the water in the main reservoir calmed, revealing a mirrored effect of the sky above.

Beyond the rim of the reservoir, Vincent was standing outside the wooden shed-like entrance to the old mineshaft. He was wearing the respirator that he found in the tool shed to help him tolerate the fumes in the mineshaft. He felt his semi-restricted breathing echo from within the mask.

In one hand, he was holding onto a high-beam Mag flashlight and in the other, a small bag of digging tools. He opened the door to the mine, turned on the flashlight, and headed into the dimly lit façade. He proceeded to walk back in time.

The light from the sun infused the entrance with a haunting glow that quickly dissipated the deeper Vincent went in. Suddenly there was a loud bang that came from the door as it slammed shut. Vincent had propped it open, and it didn't take much of a gust of wind to blow it shut. On impact, A few of the rusty nails that held the boards in place on the door gave way allowing one slat to fall out of alignment.

A single triangle beam of light was allowed through leaving only a small clue, the only clue, to give Vincent his bearings.

Vincent found himself slowly working his way deeper into the tunnel following the cone-shaped beam of light from his flashlight. He paused for a moment and panned the flashlight around to get a sense of if the tunnel was getting any smaller the deeper he went. He assessed that it was staying about the same, so he continued onward.

Vincent came to a point in the tunnel that was six feet high, and six feet wide, but the heavy posts made from oak that held the cross beams in place narrowed the width to about four feet. He traveled deeper into the tunnel. Vincent had to rely solely on the flashlight to cut through the pitch-black darkness ahead. Although the size of the tunnel was not getting any smaller, it seemed the deeper he traversed into the shaft, it felt like the walls were now closing in on him. This temporary sense of claustrophobia caused his breathing to quicken and the sound of it reverberating in the mask seemed to be louder.

Something caught Vincent's eye, so he stopped and took out a small picking tool from his bag and tapped it on a shiny piece in the sidewall of the tunnel. It didn't take much effort to loosen a small piece that fell into his hand.

"Pyrite." He told himself.

He dropped the remnants of the fake-looking gold onto the ground and where it landed, he saw there was a small pile of it already there. He didn't know if it fell from the walls on its own or if someone had made that pile many years before.

As Vincent cautiously worked his way deeper into the tunnel, the beam on his flashlight began to fade and then go bright again, giving him a sense that his mind was starting to play tricks on him as he felt like the tunnel was getting smaller.

Eventually, Vincent came to a small outcropping in the shaft. There, lying on the ground, was an old hard hat and next to it was a glass Mason jar. He panned the light around and saw what appeared to be a tin can wedged into the side of the wall. He worked the can out of the hole and discovered it was a Coors beer can from the 30's. He shoved the can back into the hole and moved on.

Deeper into the shaft, Vincent was panning the beam from the flashlight in every direction, measuring the walls and checking the beams for their integrity. There was no sign of which way was out. His breathing began to become shallower and quicker. The sound of his amplified breathing in the mask wasn't helping the situation. With the light, he located his footprints and figured if he just retraced them, it would show him the way out.

Taking in the angle of the posts and beams that were holding the walls back, they indicated to him he had been traveling in a slight downhill trajectory.

"Uphill is out." He thought to himself. "Uphill is out."

Vincent took a few more steps and remembered something. "Oh, shit."

Vincent stopped and opened the small bag he had with him. He removed a few glow sticks, cracked one, and dropped it at his feet. He then cracked another and tossed it as far back up the tunnel as he could.

Now that Vincent had a better reference of where he was, and more importantly, which way was out, his breathing began to normalize and the echo in the mask began to subside.

He sensed he feared more disappointment in himself than of Robert if he came back with nothing to show. All he needed was to find something, anything, he could bring back that could indicate to, and show Robert, he had a sense of worth and value he could bring to the table. Then he could get the finder's fee that Robert said would be enough for him to be able to pay off his debt, and the rest, stake him in the Dominion deal, to get himself whole again.

As Vincent pointed the concentrated beam further down the tunnel, he noticed the light at the end of its reach, that ground was making odd movements. It was moving.

This made Vincent even more curious about what lay ahead. He stepped on something that didn't feel like dirt or rock. He looked under his foot and saw a small rectangular shape on the dusty floor. He kicked the object, recognized what it was, and picked it up. He brushed as much of the dust off using his sleeve and he was right, an old gold-plated butane lighter. It wasn't the gold he was looking for but hoped it was a sign. He slipped it into his pocket and moved on.

The closer he got to the illusion on the floor, it became evident that what had made the light abnormal looking was that the tunnel ahead was blocked by water. His voice seemed to reverberate the sarcasm a couple of octaves lower in the mask. "Great."

Vincent retrieved another glow stick from his pouch, cracked it, gave it a good shake to help activate the chemicals in it that gave it the fluorescent glow, and tossed it as far into the tunnel as the water would allow. It ricocheted off the slant of the ceiling about twenty feet out and dropped onto the surface of the water.

When the glow stick landed, due to its buoyancy, it stayed on the surface of the water. Its glow didn't seem to penetrate the water as much as he thought it would.

Vincent wasn't happy with the outcome, "Dah."

Vincent cracked another glow stick, gave it a good shake, and used the loop on the end of the stick to attach it to the handle of the picking tool. He tossed the pick tool-glow stick combo out as far as he could. He watched the glow stick sink to the bottom which he calculated to be about five to six feet.

When the mass of the pickaxe hit the water, it caused the other glow stick that was floating on the surface, to travel in its wake to the left side of the tunnel. Now, with two glow sticks only feet apart, Vincent could see what appeared to be a silhouette of an object, a dark mass near the left side wall, between the two illuminated sticks.

Vincent moved a little closer to the water's edge to try to get a better look at the anomaly. In doing so, Vincent's foot slipped in a little bit of mud, and on into the water. He caught his balance but by then it was too late, and he was in the water halfway up his calf.

Vincent thought to himself, *in for an ounce, in for a pound.* "Oh, what the hell." He carefully waded into the water and stopped when it had reached just above his knees. He reached out but still wasn't close enough to chance losing his footing once again, so he drifted a bit further in until the water was even with his belt buckle.

The cold, slimy water was now waste deep on Vincent. With one hand on the flashlight, he reached out with the other and was able to touch the object just under the water's surface. He tried to pull up on it, but it barely moved, and he lost his grip.

Vincent regained his composure and went to take another small step but ended up sliding a bit more than expected, and the water was now up to his chest. The water was cold, and panic was starting to set in. His breathing began to speed up once again. The echoes in his mask were catching up to the trepidation he felt in his heart.

Vincent got a good grip on the object and gave a hard pull. The object moved. He braced himself as best he could and gave another hard yank.

The object moved, but so did Vincent. The object was lodged tight, causing him to slip and go underwater.

With one hand still on the object and the other holding the flashlight, Vincent aimed the light at the object. His respirator was now acting like a diving mask, and there, staring back at him, was a human skull, still attached to the rest of its skeleton.

Vincent screamed inside his mask. He felt the air bubbles escape between his skin and the rubber seal of the mask. He let go of the skeleton and in a panic, he waved the flashlight around, and then let out another scream upon seeing another smaller skeleton right next to the first one.

With no air left in his lungs, he had to find a way to resurface. His feet were slipping on the bottom, so he tried swimming but felt weighed down from his clothes and the small equipment bag he had slung over his shoulder. He swam out of the bag and tossed it onto dry land. He flipped the Mag light in the same general direction. When the light hit the ground, the light went off, leaving him in almost pitch darkness. The only light there came from a single glow stick that was floating on the surface of the water a few feet away.

It was all Vincent could do in a full-blown panic to dog paddle to the edge, crawl out of the water, and onto the dry land. He ripped off the mask to get some fresh air only to find out the air was even more rancid than what he breathed in earlier. He quickly put the mask back on and tried to clear the bad air from the mask. He reached for the flashlight and got it working.

He could taste the nightmare, "Oh, God."

With his vision blurred, he looked up as far as he could through the darkened tunnel, and saw in the distance, one of the glow sticks on the ground that he had left to indicate the way out. He pulled off his outer shirt which was now clinging to his body.

He could feel the slimy water crawling down his arms and the way it made his jeans slide across his legs as he moved. He quickly gathered his things and headed up the tunnel toward the next glow stick.

Vincent found the entrance, threw his shoulder into the old, weathered door, and busted it into pieces on his way out of the purgatory he had discovered. Next, he tossed the respirator aside and ran up the side of the hill that was the rim of the reservoir. Once he reached the top, he did not hesitate as he dove directly into the freshwater of the reservoir.

A moment later, he came up, doing his best to catch his breath. He dunked himself again and again and he ran his hands through his hair to wash the slime out of it as best he could. He pulled off his t-shirt and tossed it onto the shore. After another quick rinse, he climbed out of the reservoir and gathered his things. He took a seat on the rim of the reservoir that overlooked the broken-down entrance and stared into the nightmare of the abyss from which he came.

CHAPTER 13

Upon entering the very well-maintained grounds of the Silverado Country Club, one would take in the picturesque placement of arching palm trees, tall eucalyptus, and welcoming surroundings. The twelve-hundred-acre resort had two sprawling PGA Championship golf courses whose fairways play alongside groves of oak trees, vineyards, and luxurious condos.

Andrew Marchetti pulled his 2020 Chevy Malibu up to the valet staging area, grabbed his briefcase, then as he got out of the car took the ticket from the valet before heading up the steps toward the main entrance of the building.

As Andrew entered the foyer, he began to straighten his clothes and made sure his tie was centered, as he always wanted to make a good impression with the man he was in cahoots with, one Mr. Venturella. He walked past the check-in desk and down the steps that led into a high-ceilinged reception area. A local artist was having an auction of his paintings for a local charity that was tied into the celebrity golf tournament planned for that weekend.

On the main floor, there were dozens of paintings on display. The larger ones were on easels and the smaller ones were propped up on tabletops. The locals liked to attend this part of the charity event as a chance to mingle with celebrities who had arrived early and were bidding on the paintings.

In the middle of the showing was the artist who was trying to divide his attention between those who were seriously interested in his work and those who were there on the off chance might be caught photobombing for the local photographer who was getting a few pictures for the club's website. Next to the photographer was a journalist who was taking notes of the artists' work. She wrote: 'Huddleston's use of an organic color pallet captures the essence of the natural world and suggests a strong connection to the valley's mysticism.'

One of the pictures happened to catch Andrew's eye so he paused long enough to get a look at the bids. In the process he overheard the artist describing his use of acrylics on canvas to create landscapes done in both traditional and impressionistic styles.

The painting that caught his attention was of a vineyard with an old barn on it and an old rustic pickup truck out front. It reminded him of his grandfather's place he used to visit when he was a kid.

Opposite the painter, the was another artist who, in his golden years, took old, used, wooden golf club heads, and hand-painted them to look like birds. He hand-carved the head and neck area out of wood, glued it atop one end of the club head, then sanded it to blend into what looked like a bird, except on one side, you could still see the face of the club head. After that, he hand-painted the entire piece to look like almost any species of bird you could imagine. The locals couldn't get enough of the majestic faux-feather fowls, and they always seemed to go fast.

Andrew was about to put a bid down on one when he was interrupted by a waitress who offered him a drink. He ordered and mentioned he was meeting someone on the back patio, and he would take his drink out there.

On the backside patio that overlooked the eighteenth green of the South course, Nicolas Venturella was with a man who was on his payroll but not on his payroll. More like associates with benefits.

Transactions with deniable actions. Whatever the need, money made it bleed. That was Takata's motto. The two men were sitting at one of the umbrella tables, having an afternoon cocktail.

Nicolas drank from his Mojito and turned to his guest, "Any problems?"

Takata flipped the swizzle trick out of the Mojito and sucked down half of it with one swig. "Ahh. No problem. I let him know he was now on the hook for the whole enchilada and then some, and if he doesn't come through, I'll be taking out my disappointment on his sister. You can tell Mr. Bellacini that kid is wound so fucking tight right now he will do whatever you ask of him."

Nicolas turned to say something to Takata and saw Marchetti heading their way. With a nod of his head, he excused Takata, "That will be all for now."

Takata finished off his drink and then walked to the end of the patio and down the steps that led over to The Grill restaurant and bar to avoid running into Marchetti.

Marchetti approached the table. "Good afternoon, Mr. Venturella. I have that information you wanted."

"Are you going to stand there and announce it to everyone?" Nicolas gestured to him to take a seat.

Andrew took the empty chair left by Takata.

"What do you have for me, Andrew? Give it to me in short sentences. I don't have much time. My wife thinks I'm here to get one of Huddleston's paintings for her."

"Yeah, I saw one I…"

"She's pretty high on this local painter and I think she wants to commission him to do a landscape of Ceil Bleu."

"I think…"

"I think we should get down to business. What do you have for me?"

Andrew set his briefcase up on the table and opened it. He started to take out a file when Nicolas held out his hand causing him to pause momentarily.

"Not here," Nicolas said. "Just give me what I want to hear."

Andrew put the file away and closed the case. Just then, the server walked up with his top-shelf Margarita that he had previously ordered.

The server turned to Nicolas. "May I freshen your drink, Mr. Venturella?"

"No, thank you, but you can put his drink on my tab and close it out for me."

The server picked up the empty glass that was left by Takata.

Nicolas kept his focus on the nearby green and watched as the next foursome's approach shots landed on the green. "Tell me about the status of the lease. Are we going to have any problems with our bid to take over the Golden Dominion?"

Andrew watched the player's approach shot on the 18th green land near the flag, hop past the hole a few feet, then spin back toward the cup. As it did, it lipped out and stopped a few inches from the hole.

Nicolas got the response he wanted to hear from his inside man. "No. No problems."

Nicolas' drink arrived, he took a sip and thanked the server. "Perfect." He dropped a $10 bill on her tray and thanked her. Nicolas reached out and tapped on the briefcase. "I can trust you on this, right?"

“Trust is one thing, cash is another. As long as things stay as they are, your bid, being the first at this price, will be the accepted offer.”

The two men watched a player on the green sink a 20-foot put that rattled the bottom of the cup.

“Not to worry, when this deal goes through, you'll be compensated.” Nicolas’ cell phone rang, and he took the call. “Yes, what is it?”

*****

Among the long shadows of the late afternoon, Vincent’s face was looking off in the distance as the setting sun was getting close to finding the horizon.

“Can you tell me once again why you were in the abandoned mine in the first place?” Detective Atlock asked.

The detective’s, matter-of-fact growl in his voice brought Vincent out of his, lost in the moment in time, gaze. He turned to answer but was cut off by Nicolas in an act to protect Vincent.

“You don't have to answer any more questions, Vincent.”

“It’s okay, Mr. Venturella. Like I said, I had heard about the abandoned mine and wanted to take a look for myself. I came up to where the mine was flooded and got turned around. Then I lost my footing and slipped into the water.

Atlock was doing as detectives often do and asked the same questions in different ways hoping to find something new or to catch someone off guard in a lie. “And that's when you found the bodies?”

“Yes, Sir,” Vincent replied.

Atlock’s partner, Detective Bellmont, joined the group. “We might have an ID on one of the victims.”

“Victims,” Nicolas responded. “Who said they were victims of anything? They could have just got lost down there and we're overtaken by the rising floodwaters.”

Bellmont answered, “When the remains were taken out of the water, the smaller skeleton, we believe to be female, still had a piece of rope around one of her ankles. I was just talking to the coroner as he was examining the male skeleton. He found the tip of a knife blade lodged in one of the ribs. So, I can say within a reasonable doubt, I believe we have a double homicide.”

Detective Atlock, asked his partner, “Tell me about this I.D.”

Detective Bellmont continued where he had left off. “The female victim had a steel plate attached across her collarbone. The coroner already got a response from running the plate through the hospital's database and came back with the name, Sofia Salazar. She was listed as missing along with her husband Diego twenty years ago.”

Detective Atlock followed up, “Who reported them missing?”

“I did.”

The two detectives turned to see Father Chance, holding a Bible in his hands, standing only a few paces away. Standing next to him was Hope.

After the two detectives had a moment to talk privately to Father Chance, they took Vincent aside while everyone else gathered at the other end of the reservoir.

It was a good distance away and Nicolas was joined by Jillian and Michael. They were doing their best to put all the pieces together.

Michael kept his focus on the two detectives who were now talking to Vincent, as well as Hope, but was also talking to the group as a whole. "Do you have any idea who they were?"

Nicolas put his two cents in. "Could be workers from a collapse years ago. Your guess is as good as mine."

Robert, Bianca, and Adriana walked up behind the Venturellas.

Adriana drifted over next to Michael. Out of habit, she reached over and took his hand, and Michael did not resist the comforting gesture. "How are you feeling?"

"I'm okay."

Robert asked the group, "Any word yet on who they think it might be?"

Before anyone could give a response, they watched as Hope twisted her body in anger as she pushed away from the detectives and into Father Chance's arms.

They heard Vincent's pain as his distraught scream faded into the night, "No!..."

They saw Vincent turn away and start to run the entire length of the reservoir, but his legs could no longer carry him, and he stopped and fell to his knees.

As Vincent took solace in being alone, Hope turned and walked toward Michael. As she did, Father Chance gave Vincent his space and followed Hope.

The closer Hope got to Michael; the group could see the tears she could not hold any longer. They waited for Hope to catch her breath.

"They believe the two bodies they found are my missing mother and father."

Adriana began to ask, "I thought…"

When Michael cut her off, "Are you going to be alright?"

Hope dropped her head and tried not to start crying again. Michael let go of Adriana's hand, stepped forward, and took Hope into his arms.

Jillian put her hand on Hope's shoulder. "If you need anything, you just let me know, dear."

Adriana turned and walked back toward the house.

Michael stepped back giving Hope her space and that was when he saw Adriana, alone, making her way back to the house.

Hope looked at Jillian. "Thank you. You're very kind."

Father Chance walked up behind Hope and put his arm around her shoulders. It didn't take much for her to fall into the comfort of the man who raised her.

Robert asked Father Chance, "Are they sure about the identification? Is it really the Salazars?"

Hope found herself needing her own space and started to slowly take a walk down the long side road that looped back toward the monastery.

Father Chance paused long enough for Hope to get out of earshot of hearing his response to the group. "Yes. They have physical evidence the woman is Sofia Salazar."

Michael still had his eye on Hope as she was taking one of the hardest walks of her life. After Father Chance said what he had to say, his heart told him to go, and he went to catch up with Hope.

Father Chance went on to say, "For now, until they know otherwise, they are assuming the other body is their father, Diego."

“Do they have a cause of death?” Robert inquired.

“The detectives didn't want to speculate any more than they had to until the autopsies come back.”

The group watched as Father Chance turned back toward Hope and saw that Michael had just caught up to her and was now walking alongside her back toward the monastery.

Jillian asked Father Chance, “Is she going to be alright?”

They watched off in the distance, as Michael put his arm around Hope’s shoulder, and they made their way back in silence toward the monastery.

“Yes. She is strong in her faith, and she will find comfort there.” Father Chance changed his focus in Vincent's direction. “If you will excuse me, I need to go be with my children.”

The rest of the group said their good nights as Father Chance turned and headed up the main road toward the monastery.

Robert, Bianca, Nicolas, and Jillian all stepped aside to clear the way as the two ambulances made their way off the property with the exhumed bodies of Sofia and Diego.

After the vehicles passed, Nicolas turned to Robert. "Let me know if you hear anything."

As Nicolas and Jillian turned and walked up the road Robert replied, "Sure thing."

Once Nicolas and Jillian were a good distance away, Bianca turned to Robert with daggers in her eyes. "I thought you said the bodies would never be found."

Bianca picked up her stride, walked away from her husband, and headed toward the main house. Robert took another good look around and surveyed the chaos that was now in the midst of redefining itself.

Robert's cell phone rang, and he took the call. "Yes." He took a deep breath. "Yes, it's true. They just discovered two bodies in an old mineshaft. Is that going to affect the buyout?" Robert shook his head. "I don't know exactly how far into the mine. Why?"

Robert didn't like what he heard and hung up the phone. He gripped the phone like he was trying to choke the life out of it as he turned and started to walk back toward the main house.

CHAPTER 14

Just as the sun was about to set, Michael and Hope were coming around the far side of the monastery having taken the longer pathway home. Michael took Hope by the hand and walked alongside her as they made their way up the few steps leading to the front porch. Once there, they each took a seat on either side of a small table.

They could hear Vincent's raised voice coming from inside the monastery, but it was hard to make out what he was saying. A moment later, Vincent walked out of the monastery, carrying a bottle of wine that had already been opened, and slammed the door behind him. He glanced over and saw Hope and Michael off to the side. Without saying a word, he headed toward the steps.

Hope could see the pain he was in, "Vincent!" Vincent stopped at the top of the stairs. "We need to talk."

"About what? About the lies we've been fed all our lives?"

Hope stood up, walked over to Vincent, and embraced him. "We are still family." She leaned back and looked Vincent in the eyes. "And that includes Father Chance."

Right then, as if on cue, Father Chance pushed open the heavy mahogany doors of the monastery and stood in the frame of the doorway.

Vincent felt there were no words Hope nor Father Chance could say to change the way he was feeling. “This whole place is based on a lie. My whole life has been a lie! If you want to keep believing, be my guest.”

Father Chance spoke from his heart, “If that is what you truly believe, I must have failed you, and for that, I am truly sorry. If you can give me a minute to explain…”

“I gave you twenty years to explain! Why should I believe you now?”

Vincent took his bottle of wine and turned his back on everything he once believed, and he headed down the path that led to the main road.

Hope called out to Vincent and started to go after him.

“Let him go, Hope.” Hope paused knowing Father Chance was probably right and took solace in his words. “There is nothing you can say right now that will ease his pain. Let him breathe on his own and maybe he will find his faith once again.”

Father Chance went to the top of the steps and put out his hand. Hope turned, put her hand in his, and together they walked over to the seating area.

Hope had desperation in her voice, "Is there anything we can do to save the monastery?"

Father Chance took a deep breath, removed the medallion from around his neck, and held it in his hands. Michael and Hope watched as he studied the medallion. They watched as he took apart the two remaining pieces and then linked them back together.

"When I was given this medallion, I was told it was the key to the survival of the monastery and the land the vineyard is on, and to never let it out of my possession." Once again, he separated the pieces and then linked them back together. "I took it figuratively." He looked closer into the details near the center of the medallion. "What if, it actually is a key to something?"

Michael concluded, "Then we're going to need the other piece of the medallion."

"Yes, Michael. I think you're right." Father Chance replied.

Hope saw something in his eyes. "What is it? What do you see, Father?"

"It's not what I see in the medallion, it's what the monsignor said before he passed away. *The Brother's Secret.* When I took over as curator of the monastery, I was given a book that had pages falling out of it. I was so focused on the loose pages at the time that I didn't go back and read the rest of the book until many years later."

"What was the secret?" Michael asked. "Do you still have the book?

"I'm not sure. I'll be right back."

Father Chance went inside the monastery and went into his room. He began scanning the floor-to-ceiling bookshelf. Eventually, he found the book and then returned to the front porch. "Here it is. Somewhat still intact." He took a seat at the table and began to carefully fan through the pages. "Here's what I remember of what the monsignor told me. Four monks were in charge of the reconstruction of the monastery in the early 30's. The fire had taken most of the wooden building to the ground; so, they decided to replace it, using stone. It took them three years."

"Why so long? Was it just the four of them?" Hope asked.

"As far as I could tell, yes. They each had their own personal skills and only used extra labor when needed."

Hope picked up one of the loose pages from the book. She saw a partial drawing of what looked like a set of internal gears for a clock. "Do you know what these drawings mean?"

"Most of them are just partial drawings. They look like plans of some kind. What I did find, that is starting to make sense now, is four names." Father Chance pulled out a page with a list of names. "These are the names of the four monks and their particular skill sets. There was a Father Sebastian who was the stonemason, Father Daniel who was a carpenter, Father Gregory who was a blacksmith, and Father Richard who was a metallurgist."

"That's interesting," Michael said.

Father Chance agreed. "Yes, it is. Why these four monks? They were all assigned to the monastery after the fire. Why then?"

Hope turned over the page she was holding and saw a date. 1934. "This page is definitely from that time period."

Michael was thumbing through a couple of pages as well. “Here’s something. All four monks were permanently reassigned to stay and work the land after the completion of the monastery in 1936.”

Father Chance took the pages from Michael and looked them over. “I can’t find anything else here that makes any sense, so I guess whatever the Brother’s Secret was, they took whatever it was with them to their graves.”

*****

Vincent found himself walking aimlessly under the pale moonlight and paused long enough to take a swig off the bottle of wine. He knew the wine wasn't the answer and was about to throw the bottle into the distance when he saw a silhouette of someone sitting on the front steps of the Bellacini mansion.

Vincent had a good idea who it was and rather than waste a good bottle of wine he headed in her direction. He approached Adriana and raised the open bottle as a peace offering. She nodded and he took a seat next to her.

Adriana was feeling her pain. “There isn't enough wine bottled on this property to make me forget this day.”

“I found my missing parents’ remains in an abandoned mineshaft today. How are we going to top that?”

Vincent handed Adriana the bottle of wine and she took a small sip.

“I've been sleeping with my fiancée’s father for a few months, and I just found out, I'm pregnant.”

“And the winner is?”

Adriana handed the bottle of wine back to Vincent. “At this point, it doesn’t matter. No one loves me.”

“What do you mean? How could that be?”

“One’s married and the other one can’t remember why he wants to marry me.”

Vincent took a swig of courage. “Fools, both of them.”

Adriana saw the way Vincent was looking at her. It was the way he saw right into her heart and the only way that could have happened was if, at this moment in time, both walls they had each built to protect themselves from the rest of the world, had come crumbling down. She saw the pain in his eyes from having fought so hard for so long and had finally been set free.

“So, does that make us both winners or both losers?”

“No one wins around here except for my father. I've seen what he'll do to justify what he wants, including taking the monastery for himself.”

“I thought he was in a partnership with Venturella on that one.”

Vincent took another sip from the bottle before he handed it back to Adriana, who in turn, took another swig.

“You don't know my father.”

“But he said, if I got him the silver medallion, I would get a percentage of the take.”

“What take?”

“The silver mine,” Vincent replied.

“There is no silver mine. Don't you get that? He had heard about the medallion and wanted you to steal the one thing that had any real value to Father Chance.”

Vincent put his head in his hands. Adriana tapped him on the side of his arm with the bottle of wine. Vincent waved her off.

“What have I done?” Vincent turned enough to face Adriana. “Do you know where your father is keeping the silver piece of the medallion?”

“There's no way you're getting close to that.”

Vincent, in haste to stand up and head down the steps, accidentally knocked the bottle of wine from Adriana’s hand. The bottle rolled down the last few steps pouring out the last of the wine.

“Vincent.” Something in the way Adriana said his name gave him pause. “If it means that much to you, come back tomorrow.”

Vincent leaned down, picked up the empty wine bottle, and poured out its last few drops. He looked into Adriana’s eyes, shrugged his shoulders, turned, and headed back up the road.

CHAPTER 15

Workers were pruning the vines in the parcel that was within the large circle drive in front of the main house. One of the workers paused long enough to take out a sandstone and began to sharpen his pruning knife. Once he thought the knife was ready, he picked up an old piece of vine from a pile of discarded branches and tested the knife's newly sharpened edge. With a flick of his wrist, he cut through the small branch like it was butter.

From inside Robert's office, from behind her father's desk, Adriana had been watching the workers trimming the vines in the center of the circle drive. Adriana went back over to the door, took off her earbuds, and checked the hallway. She saw no signs of her father. She closed the door but left a small gap, just enough so she could hear if he was coming back up the stairs. She knew she didn't have much time and made her way over to the large black leather chair behind the desk.

On the corner of her father's desk was a handcrafted one-of-a-kind cigar box. The bottom portion of the box had a small drawer with a silver knob on it.

She tried to open the drawer, but it would not move, then she remembered that the lid had to be opened first. Once she opened the drawer, she saw that it contained a cigar cutter and a small key.

Adriana removed the key and unlocked the top center drawer of the desk. Inside the drawer, Robert had wrapped the silver portion of the medallion in a silk handkerchief. She removed the handkerchief and set it in the middle of the desk. She slowly tossed back the corners of the loosely wrapped hankey, exposing the silver portion of the medallion. She lifted the handcrafted design of silver and felt its misleading weight. It was lighter than she thought. She angled the piece trying to get a better look at the inlaid jewels. She spun the desk chair around to face the window so she could use the natural light to get a better look at the stones. They seemed to come to life as the light of the afternoon sun shimmered off them. She admired the small little details right down to the way the prongs held each jewel in place and the way the light bounced off the four precision-cut stones. Two of the stones were solid. The other two allowed the sunlight to pass through causing a mesmerizing rainbow effect.

Adriana looked out the window and saw one of the workers watching her. She quickly became paranoid at the thought he could see what she was holding and turned the chair back around. When she spun around, she ended up bumping the computer's mouse. This woke the screen up and she noticed an icon she hadn't noticed before. She clicked on it. To her surprise, it opened. There was a series of files with hyphenated names and among them were: YTD, Ex, VHS Xfers, Pics, GDL, and one marked, A&N.

Adriana decided to start with VHS Xfers. She clicked on the file, and it opened to a subfile. There were a series of video clips. She opened one labeled: Bianca. The recording showed Bianca at her Quinceanera, the celebration of her fifteenth birthday that was being held on the grounds of the Bellacini vineyard. She clicked on the sound icon and could hear children's laughter and the voices of the attending guests. She recognized Alejandro's voice saying, "La bella Bianca es ahora una mujer."

Adriana was a bit taken as she heard Alejandro say, "Beautiful Bianca is now a woman."

Adriana clicked on Pics. A folder opened with a series of pictures of Bianca from age fifteen to her early twenties. Each picture tells a story. Starting with the shy fifteen-year-old and moving on to the more flirtatious ones. Then there was a series of pictures of her going through her pregnancy starting at age seventeen. In the background of a few of the pictures was Alejandro. He was smiling in some and somber in others. When she saw a picture of an urn with the same date as her mother's birthday, she was reminded of the story that her mother had told her of the day her mother was born, that Bianca's mother, her grandmother, Benedetta, had passed giving birth to Bianca. Then she saw a picture that stood out. It was a polaroid of Alejandro holding her as a newborn baby at the hospital. Someone had written on the label below the picture: Nina Adriana con abuela.

Adriana clicked out of the Pics file and slid the cursor over to the file marked: A&N. She paused for a moment, then clicked on it. A dozen small boxes popped up across the screen. Each box was a small picture of a room she recognized but not necessarily from this angle. She clicked on one of the boxes. The box zoomed out to a three-quarter size version of the screen, and a video started to play.

The image on the screen was not from her iPhone. There on the screen was a view from a higher angle overlooking a bed. Not just any bed, but the bed she and Nicolas Venturella had been sharing. She knew her father was aware of their affair and would have her leave her iPhone propped up and recording but there were also times when she wanted the more explicit times with Nicolas to herself.

This angle of their time together was different. From this angle, Adriana could see her phone face down on the nightside table.

Adriana was completely unaware her father had been making his own recordings and to what end he would use them. She knew of the blackmail scheme to keep Nicolas at bay with his desire to one day take over the Golden Dominion, but why would he not tell her? What was he planning to do with these recordings against her?

From this angle of the recording, Adriana had figured the camera had to have been hidden up on the corner shelf among the knickknacks Nicolas had collected over the years from various vineyards up and down the valley.

The room itself was a bit bare. Except for the bed and end table, that was about it, except for a small dinette table next to the window that overlooked a courtyard. The room was one of two bedrooms in the guesthouse that was located on the far side of the property. It was currently under renovation and had been for a couple of years, they referred to it as, the chateau.

Adriana became voyeuristic and fascinated by what she was watching. She saw the way her body was outlined under a beige silk sheet as it flowed over her silhouette. She saw Nicolas appear from the bathroom only wearing a towel around his waist. She remembered that night. Using the mouse, she once again clicked on the sound.

She heard Nicolas ask, "Did you take my last razor?"

Adriana drew back the sheet and exposed herself all the way down to her thighs. "I'm sorry. I needed it."

Nicolas saw nothing but bare skin. "Apology accepted." Nicolas removed his towel and used it to wipe away the shaving cream from his face then tossed the towel aside.

Adriana continued to watch the recording as he laid her face down on the bed, followed by the way he began to kiss her slowly from the back of her neck down to her lower back. It was as if she was having an out-of-body experience but at the same time, she was having flashbacks of divine tenderness as if she could still feel his lips on her warm skin.

Adriana ran her hand on the back of her neck as if having the sense of a sensual memory come rushing back to her in full splendor.

The sound. She forgot the sound was on!

She quickly muted the recording and then closed the video file. She decided to click on another one. This one was different. It was not at the beginning of the recording but near the end. It was of her and Nicolas lying in each other's arms. Their bodies entwined and sweat was dripping off them both as they were both still lost in the euphoria of passion.

Then it hit her, this was from just last week. She caught her breath and used the cursor to slide the tracking indicator back a couple of minutes.

She saw herself in the middle of the bed, on her knees, biting down on a swath of bed sheet while her hands were trying to stay gripped on the edge of the bed as Nicolas was on his knees behind her. They were in total rhythm bringing her close to a climax.

Adriana wanted to hear Nicolas expressing his love for her once again, so she turned the sound back on, but this time on low. She heard herself and her lover moaning. Then she heard herself begging him not to stop. As if on cue, they held each other tightly, and then their bodies began to shudder as one. She let out a deeply pent-up moan that had been waiting for a breath of fresh air to give it life.

Adriana realized this was the point where her father had been watching the video before he shut it off. She stopped the recording in the same place and clicked the speaker icon to off, and it was just in time. She heard a creak on the stairs followed by her father's voice as he must have been talking to someone on his cell phone. Just before he reached the top of the stairs, she heard him clearly say, “All this has to go away.”

Adriana quickly closed the series of files she had unlocked and then put the computer back in sleep mode. She slipped the empty silk scarf back into the top drawer of the desk, locked it, and then slipped the key back into its hiding place.

Out in the hallway, Robert stopped at the top of the stairs. His attention was on his call, and he hadn't noticed that Bianca was standing in front of the entry to the den that was located just below the landing he was on. Not only could Adriana hear the conversation, but so did Bianca.

Robert boasted, "The police only know what we tell them." Then he hung up the phone.

Just before Robert was going to enter his office, both Robert and Adriana heard her mother's voice.

Bianca emerged from the room opposite Robert's office. "Robert, we need to talk."

Robert stopped midstride with his hand on the doorknob. He turned to face Bianca.

Bianca continued, "We have a busy season coming up and I'd like to bring my uncle's family…"

"Enough about your family!"

"They're your family, too!"

"No." He paused, "They're not. Just because I agreed to help them get their immigration status, doesn't make them family. Just like anyone else, if they don't pull their share of the work, they're gone."

"Even my father?"

Adriana was caught totally off guard. She got up from the desk and stood closer to the door.

Robert gave Bianca a cold look. "I told you, if Adriana ever finds out about Alejandro being her grandfather, the deals off."

"Robert, the deal is, you have another child on the way."

"I told you, the only name that matters around here is Bellacini."

"So, I guess I don't matter to you at all? Robert, I know why we never married."

Robert's expression went cold.

Bianca elaborated, "I found the divorce papers from your ex-wife that you never signed. I found something else. She's now living in Calistoga with a real estate developer and, according to the website they seem to be doing quite well for themselves."

"You know if I sign those papers, I lose this vineyard. This land is Bellacini land, family, or no family."

"You better not ever let your daughter hear you say that."

Adriana looked back over at the desk and realized she had left the medallion out. She quickly sat back behind the desk, placed the silver medallion in her lap, put her earbuds back in, and slid herself up close to the desk.

Robert saw his daughter sitting in his favorite chair at his desk. He ended the call on his cell phone and turned his attention to Adriana. "May I help you?"

Adriana removed her earbuds. "What?"

"What-do-you-want?"

"I need your advice on something."

Robert sensed he wasn't going to like what he was about to hear, walked over to his wet bar, and poured himself a glass of water from a lead crystal pitcher that he got as a gift for his anniversary... which one, he couldn't remember.

As he was pouring the water with his back to Adriana, she hid the silver piece of the medallion in the only place she could. She slipped it up under her skirt and put the triangle section of the medallion inside the front of her panties.

Robert took a sip of water and then headed back over to his desk. “Do you mind?”

Adriana got up out of her father's chair and walked around to one of the chairs that faced the front of the desk as he took back what he considered to be his throne.

Robert reached into the cigar box and grabbed a fresh cigar. He slid open the lower drawer, removed the stainless-steel cigar cutter, and clipped the end of his cigar. After a couple of good puffs to get the cigar going well, “What kind of advice are you looking for?”

“How do you feel about becoming a grandfather?”

Robert almost choked on the deep inhale as he sat up quickly in his chair, “I would say that is bad timing now that it looks like you and Michael may not be on the way to the altar.”

“Did I say it was Michael’s?”

Just outside the door, out of sight, was Bianca, waiting to hear his answer.

Robert took a long sip of water to clear his throat. "I asked you to sleep with Nicolas to keep me informed of his intentions on the buyout, not to fall in love with him and have his baby for God's sake!"

"Just so you know, at this point, it's not like it would make a difference. Business is business, right Daddy?"

Adriana got up and walked out of the office. As she did, she closed the door behind her. Just as the door closed, from the hallway, Adriana could hear a water glass being shattered up against the wall near the office door.

Adriana made her way down the stairs, and as she did, Bianca slowly opened the door of the master bedroom that was located across the hallway from Robert's office. Bianca walked over to the office and was about to open the door when she paused with her hand over the doorknob. She decided instead of confronting Robert, she would turn and head down the stairs.

From his office, Robert saw Adriana as she walked down the right side of the circle drive past Alejandro and his team as they continued to trim the vines. Robert turned to see one of the housekeepers standing in the doorway of his office. He gestured at the broken glass on the ground, "Can you clean that up?" Robert caught his bad demeanor toward the maid and semi-apologized with a sarcastic, "Please."

As the woman entered his office, he didn't bother looking where he was walking and stepped through the broken glass and tracked some of it out the door.

Just as Robert was about to open the front door, he felt his foot stick in place and realized he had a shard of glass in his shoe that had been leaving scratches in the wood floor of the foyer. He tried to knock it loose but all he did was add more grooves to the already disfigured floor. He made his way onto the front porch and walked over to the front edge where he scraped the bottom of his shoe and dislodged the piece of glass. He kicked the shard to the side and off the top step into the rose bushes.

At this point Robert didn't want to think about family, he just wanted to refocus on his plan to acquire Golden Dominion.

He entered between the first and second row of vines where the workers were currently trimming. He made his way past a few of the migrants, past a small work cart, and then walked up to where Alejandro was supervising his men.

Robert grabbed a handful of grapes, crushed a couple of them between his fingertips, smelled the juices, and then tasted its sugar content.

Alejandro knew what Robert wanted to know, so he took a few grapes and did the same. “I think we are close, Senor. I think a week, maybe two, no more.”

Back behind the work cart, a couple of workers paused what they were doing, and stepped aside.

Bianca reached over and took a pruning knife away from one of the workers.

Robert’s attention was still engaged with Alejandro. “If the weather continues like it's been, we should have a better harvest than last year.”

Robert saw Alejandro’s reaction to someone walking up behind Robert. Robert turned around to see who it was.

Before Robert could say a word, he felt the blade of the pruning knife that Bianca had just wielded slice across his gut from left to right. A massive amount of excruciating pain caused Robert to become instantly disoriented and lose all track of the concept of time. A euphoric high one second and his nerves on fire the next. He dropped to his knees and felt a most unnatural feeling. He reached down and tried to keep his life from falling out of him.

Robert looked up at Bianca. It was her vengeful eyes that were the last thing he saw as she wielded the pruning knife blade back in the opposite direction, which sliced open his throat.

Bianca's midsection had a blood spray across it from her first slice across Robert's belly and was now getting sprayed once again from the main arterial spray from Robert's throat.

Robert's hands dropped to his side as he sat dead on his knees.

The field workers were all stunned at the site of what had just happened and didn't know what to do. They watched as Bianca, unfazed, spat on the ground, turned, and walked back toward the main house.

Robert's body had lost all tension in its mass and fell forward into the dirt, with a thud.

Bianca walked past the work cart. As she did, she handed the worker back his pruning knife, then headed back toward the house as if what just happened was all in a day's work.

CHAPTER 16

The Christ figure that hung on the cross above the altar had the traditional indication of where Casca Longinus, the Roman soldier, had stabbed Jesus in his side. There was a stain of blood below and in the wound at his side.

At the altar, Father Chance was looking through his leather-bound King James version of the Holy Bible that had been on the altar ever since the monastery was built. “Look here.”

Michael and Hope moved closer to get a better look.

Father Chance showed them one of the first pages of the Bible. Each side of the page had a hand-painted articulate design. On one side, was an image of Eden with vines all along the outer edge of the page. As he turned the page, the other side showed an image of Hell with streams of molten rock along the outer edge of the page.

Father Chance took the outside edge of the page and, without creasing it, carefully folded it back so the right side of the Eden image on the underside of the page was now lined up near the right side of the Hell page.

There, among the swirling vines was a rough image of the medallion. Also, running down the left side, there was a combined image of the sweeping molten lava on the right, and when the two images were aligned, a word could be seen running down the page. Mazzaroth.

Michael had a bad angle and had to ask, “It looks like it says Mazza something. Does that mean anything to you?”

Father Chance knew exactly what it said and the meaning behind it. “Mazzaroth. It's from the book of Job and means, The Garland of Crowns.”

Hope thought she knew her scriptures well but wasn't quite sure of the reference. “As in?”

Father Chance had heard the stories that had been handed down but before his predecessor could explain the true meaning behind the clue that was left behind, he had passed away.

“A celestial journey. In this case, a celestial treasure.”

Michael wanted to confirm he heard Father Chance correctly, “A treasure?”

Hope got a sense of where Father Chance was going with this. "As in the crown of thorns like the one Christ had worn during his crucifixion?"

"Exactly." Father Chance replied.

Michael interjected, "Are you talking about the actual crown of thorns Pontius Pilate put on Christ's head?"

"Yes and no. Yes, it wasn't Pilot who placed the thorns on his head but as governor, he was the one who ordered the Roman soldiers to place a purple robe on Jesus' body and the crown of thorns to mock him as a king."

Both Michael and Hope looked up at the figure of Christ that hung on the cross beyond the altar.

Hope lets out a heavy sigh. "And to think he was arrested and came before the religious court of the High Priest. They could not find anything within his teaching to condemn him, so they found someone to bear false witness just to charge him with a crime."

Michael looked at the crown upon the head of Jesus in a new light and saw how the thorns had drawn blood. He, without thinking about it, brought his hand up to his head and touched his scalp about where the crown lay upon the head of Jesus.

Hope saw the wonder in Michael and finished her thought. "The thorns were said to have a toxin in them that then spread the poison throughout his body."

Michael didn't even remember saying the words. "The pain."

Father Chance reaffirmed. "Yes, he was in pain. Imagine being beaten, poisoned, and made to carry a cross made of pine that weighed 165 pounds through the streets while being mocked, spat upon, and stoned along the way. He was then nailed to the cross around 9 in the morning and that afternoon around 3, with his last breath he called out, "Father, into your hands I commit my spirit."

Without a word being said, the room went quiet as if they were all asked to pray.

After a moment they all raised their heads. Michael noticed Hope wiping a tear from her cheek. Hope noticed Michael looking her way and she gave him just a slight smile. In return, Michael could see the beauty not only in her smile but in her eyes.

Vincent broke the silence, "…and…?"

"No, I don't think it's the actual crown. The last I heard it was under seal in the Notre Dame cathedral in Paris." Father Chance studied the hidden clue within the artwork. "I now believe this is a reference to something else."

"Why do you say that?" Hope asked.

Father Chance pointed to a single word that was also formed within the vines. "Ophir."

Michael asked, "What does that mean?"

Before Father Chance could respond Vincent had the answer. "It's not a what but a where. Ophir is a region of wealth mentioned in Kings. Mainly for its export of gold in the time of Solomon."

"So, you're saying there just might be a crown made of gold hidden somewhere here in the monastery?" Michael asked.

Vincent's heart began to race. "There's got to be. Why would they go through all this trouble to hide clues that only a man of faith could follow?"

Michael and Father Chance looked at one another.

Father Chance made a general comment for the group but mainly toward Michael. "And it's going to take a man with faith to find it."

Michael had to ask, "Father, do you know where it is?"

Father Chance took a good look around the inside of the monastery. He opened his arms wide and turned back toward Hope and Michael. "All I know is, I am on the same journey as you. I was told that everything in this monastery was to remain in place at all times, and I am assuming it was for a very good reason."

From the altar, Hope took a good look around the inside the monastery at all the stained glass, every statue, and every painting. "So, if a crown of gold does exist, does that mean if we can find it, it might be worth enough that we will be able to save the vineyard?"

Father Chance looked around and his gaze eventually came back to Hope. "It could be a start but…"

Hope interjected, "But what?"

"I just don't want to get your hopes up. First, we would need to find the crown and then some, in order to satisfy the buyout of this land."

Michael took another look at the icon on the inner lining of the Bible Father Chance had found earlier that referenced the medallion. "That being said, according to this symbol, we're going to need the entire medallion to have a chance of locating the crown."

Father Chance confirmed the reality they were all facing. His words were for all to hear but he knew it was Vincent who was feeling the weight he was carrying for his transgression. "He's right, Hope. Unless we can retrieve the rest of the medallion, we may never find out even if such a treasure truly does exist."

Father Chance could see the dejection in the way Vincent carried himself as he turned away from the group and slowly made his way out of the monastery.

Each step he took on the way down, felt as if he was descending into hell itself. Then he realized that ever since he took the silver piece of the medallion, he felt he was already there and had no one else to blame but himself.

*****

Vincent's walk had drawn him back through his own purgatory where he thought for a moment, he had hope but instead found only despair. Hell on Earth. The place that held the answer to a question that, at one time, he thought would fill his heart full of joy but instead felt like a knife that pierced his soul.

Vincent took a seat on the edge of the reservoir and took in the sun's warmth. He felt what light breeze there was, blow across his face. He couldn't take his eyes off the old wooden shack that had led to the discovery of his parents' demise.

Vincent laid back and closed his eyes for only a minute when he thought he recognized Adriana's voice.

"I thought I'd find you here." Adriana sat down next to Vincent. "I'm sorry to hear what happened to your parents."

“Thanks.” Vincent sat up and turned to Adriana, “I realized I'm not mad at Father Chance for not telling me and Hope about them, as much as, not knowing if they were still alive. It turns out, he was in the dark about it as much as Hope and I were.”

“I heard my father telling someone years ago when they put that reservoir in, that they collapsed one of the old mines, and caused some flooding.”

“So, you still think it was an accident?” Vincent saw a blank look on Adriana’s face. “Didn't you hear, they found evidence my mother's feet had been bound and my father had been stabbed?”

Adriana growled under her breath.

Vincent could see her clenching her gut. “What is it?”

The dreaded hatred Adriana felt was like a chill that ran through her body. “Nothing happens on this land without my father knowing about it.”

“So, do you think he had something to do with the death of my parents?”

“I’m not saying that…”

“Then what are you saying?”

“To be honest, at this point, I don’t know anything for sure.” For Adriana to say those words was almost a relief to finally get them off her chest. It was like going to confession but never actually having to tell the whole truth.

“How could I ever have gotten involved with your father? I should have never taken that silver medallion.”

“Why did you?” Adriana replied.

Vincent laid back down and covered his face with his hands. “I thought if I could raise some money, I could help Father Chance get the vineyard back in operation.”

“What did you think would happen when Father Chance found out?”

“There was no finding out. I took the silver medallion directly from him and walked away.”

“He gave it to you?”

“No.”

“Vincent…” Adriana felt his shame. “Why?”

"Your father said if I could help him to prove the silver came from this region it would go a long way to raising the value of the medallion itself and he would stake me a percentage of the Dominion deal. Then he could help me to maybe buy some time with the guys I was in debt with." Vincent paused and after hearing his confession to Adriana out loud, he did feel the shame of it all. "The day of Michael's accident, I was down at the marina to score a loan from a guy I had met through your father. I got the money, but Robert said I wouldn't see a return until after the buyout. Now the loan is due, and I have nothing."

"Those guys probably work for my father and from that point on, he had you in his pocket. How much?"

"A lot."

Adriana laid back on the ground alongside Vincent. She reached up under her skirt and into her panties. She removed the silver piece of the medallion and put it between the sun and Vincent's face. The sun's rays passed through a couple of the stones and sent the tinted rays of light onto the back of his hands. He caught a glimpse of the flickers of light as the defused rays passed between his fingers.

He moved his hands away and saw the source of the tinted flickers of light that had caught his attention. There in front of him, he saw the silhouette of the silver medallion and the way a couple of the stones were bending the sun's light as it passed through them.

"Maybe this will help?"

"How did you get it back?"

"The question is, what are you going to do with it?"

"The question is, what are you going to do when your father finds out you took it?"

"Once it's stolen, it's stolen. How could it be stealing if it wasn't his to begin with? That would be a bit redundant, don't you think? Besides, with my father, enough never seems to be enough."

Vincent reached out and Adriana handed him the one-third section of the medallion that was made of pure silver. Once in his hands he quickly sat up and Adriana followed.

"Why are you willing to risk helping me? You know the buyout is clearly in your family's favor. If it gets out about the source of the medallion having been mined from this land, it could delay the sale of the property and not only change the outcome of the sale but the true value, costing your father millions."

"Believe me, I've asked myself the same question almost every day. I've come to realize I've been fucked over by my father in more ways than one."

"I could kiss you right now."

"Slow your roll there, mister. I'm already in a heap of trouble."

*****

Sprinklers were spraying water on the vineyard where the workers had just finished trimming and Bianca had wielded her power over her land. Amid the light spray of the water, a rainbow could be seen, but unlike a pot of gold at the end, there was only Robert's blood being diluted into the softened wet ground.

An unmarked police car drove down the lane and entered the circle drive. Bianca stepped off the porch wearing a brightly colored sundress that was covered by an apron that accented her pregnancy. She greeted the detectives as their car came to a stop and they exited their vehicle. With a straight poker face, Bianca asked, “How may I help you?”

“We're here to speak with your husband, Mr. Bellacini.”

Behind the detectives was a large backhoe driven by Alejandro that was on its return trip from the back forty with empty bags of lye flopping around in its front loader.

Bianca went on to explain to the detectives, “He’s not here right now. I’m not sure when he will be back.” She changed her tone to let them know she was the one in charge. “How can I help you?”

“We are here to ask, what do you know about the Golden Dominion land purchase your husband is involved in?”

CHAPTER 17

The monastery was rebuilt with its foundation aligned to have the back wall behind the altar face toward the West to capture the night sky as it changed from the lighter hints of yellow, then transitioning into orange, on into the darker blues, and then eventually to the deep richness of purple. The rich colors combined with the naturally flawed textures in the stained glass that faced the setting sun, would highlight the skilled craftsmanship that was put into the spiritual artwork itself.

Father Chance was standing near the altar. As the sun's rays passed through the stained-glass windows, it cast an aura around him, leaving him in a silhouette similar to, but less intense than the religious icon behind him. As he knelt below the enlightened Christ figure, it became the designed focal point as it was meant to be.

Michael took a closer look at the piece of the medallion that was made of copper that Father Chance was holding while Hope was appreciating the intricacies of the piece that was made of gold.

Father Chance reached out and Hope passed on the one made of gold to him. Once again, he linked them together and compared the design to the symbology that had been drawn on the inside cover of the Bible lying open on the altar.

Father Chance had a heavy heart but had come to believe in miracles. He took a seat on the top step of the altar for a moment to collect his thoughts. He felt that God had a hand in saving his life and considered that to have been no small feat in the scheme of things. "Now all we need is the missing piece."

They all heard the metallic latch on the front door slide, followed by the glow of light that was created around Vincent as he entered the monastery.

Father Chance stood and greeted Vincent with a nod acknowledging his acceptance of what he had done. He was taking responsibility and returning the missing pendant. Vincent walked up to him and handed over the silver medallion. As he did, he looked up at Father Chance who was a few steps above him in front of the altar, just off center, in line with the Christ figure on the cross over his shoulder.

Although Vincent's words were meant for Father Chance, the same could have been said to the man who was impaled on the cross before him, who had sacrificed so much. “Forgive me.”

Father Chance added the silver third of the medallion to the other two pieces making it whole once again.

Hope put her hand on Vincent's shoulder and without saying a word she let her eyes thank her brother for returning what he knew was not rightfully his. Then she gave him another look that was meant to let him in on a secret as she directed her question to Father Chance. “You said you had something to show us?”

Father Chance gestured to Michael as he spoke. “Lock the main doors. What I'm about to share with you must stay between us in this room.”

Michael crossed the room, closed the doors, and slid the large two-foot-long wooden dowel through the inner handles to lock the heavy wooden doors from the inside.

After Michael rejoined the others at the altar, Father Chance went on to explain the connection he thought he had uncovered. “I was given the task to watch over these grounds and all that it protects. This medallion is just one of the keys that is needed to guard the Mazzaroth.”

Michael was about to ask for the reference, but Hope got the question out before he could find the words. “What does that mean?”

“It means, they knew what we were asked to protect was too much for one man and that danger would follow. If it got into the wrong hands, it was worth not risking the word getting out to save it.”

It clicked personally with Vincent. “It must be worth a lot whatever it is if the original monks who built this place were willing to go to such lengths to hide its location.”

Hope asked Father Chance, “Does this mean you know where the crown is?”

“No, but I do know where to begin. I recently came across something that gave me insight into where we should begin looking.”

Michael was on edge as much as Hope. “And where is that?”

“Why, in the scriptures, of course.”

Father Chance turned around and moved in front of the oversized Bible that was laid open on the altar. He flipped a few pages and found the book of John. "John fourteen says, I am the way…"

Hope responded, "And the truth and the life."

Everyone looked up at the large cross with the life-size rendering of Christ impaled on the cross. They all seem to notice about the same time that Christ, unlike in many images of him on the cross, there were very few of him looking upward, specifically in this case, at the ceiling in the center of the monastery.

Vincent followed the sightline of where Jesus was looking and determined, "If he is showing the way, the way must be found in the fresco that's painted on the ceiling."

On the ceiling of the monastery was an exquisitely hand-painted fresco of the artwork known as: Heaven and Earth. The Angel's robe was painted with light blue and green pastels that were pleasing to the eye. Her hair was blonde, and she had wings that looked as if they were made of glass.

From behind, the sun's rays accented everything about her. She seemed to be floating, but at the same time was held by the hand of God. She was levitating above the Earth while looking down, as if waiting for whoever needed her, to just ask, and she would be by their side.

From where everyone was standing, it appeared the Angel in the painting was looking directly back at them.

Michael, in the past, hadn't taken the time to study the richness or to look for the meaning of the hand-painted fresco or even how long it must have taken to do the work. "Do you know who painted the image or how long that painting has been there?"

Father Chance tried to clarify, "I was never told who painted it or even if, in our case, that would make a difference. As far as I know, it's been there from the very beginning of when this monastery was designed and built."

"Do you think the monks could have painted it?" Michael asked.

"You mean like some kind of clue?" Vincent inquired.

“Yeah, like a clue.” Michael continued his train of thought. “If the clue is in the fresco, how will we recognize it? What exactly are we looking for?”

Father Chance was always one to try to use every situation to give meaning, to teach a life lesson through scripture. “Have faith in what your heart sees and let your soul speak to you. Listen, there are lessons to be learned within the silence. Breathe in what life has to show you and appreciate the gifts it has to offer.” Michael took a deep breath. “When you exhale, let all distractions fade away and what is left, can have meaning.”

Michael exhaled. He listened to his breathing and then couldn't help but focus on the Angel’s piercing blue eyes. “It looks as if she is looking right through me and into my soul.”

Father Chance’s response touched Michael deeply. “Now you are listening. What else do you see?”

“Her hands.”

“What about her hands?”

Although they are open, she seems to be…praying. She is praying.”

"And in this instance, what prayer comes to mind?"

Michael turned to Father Chance and gave the only response he could as it was the only prayer he knew in its entirety. "The Lord's prayer."

They all began to recite the Lord's prayer to themselves hoping to find a clue within its meaning, beyond its general text.

Hope was the first to respond to what she thought it could mean. "On Earth as it is in Heaven." She continued to verbally work out her reasoning. "She's not looking at you Michael, she's looking at the floor. The earth. She's looking at the floor of the church!"

Father Chance removed the decanter of wine from the altar. He poured some of the wine in the same spot where Michael had accidentally spilled his wine earlier. Father Chance had noticed the combination of colors in the tile but hadn't linked it to their quest until now. When he did, he revealed the rest of the six-inch blue tile.

In the center of the blue tile was a two-inch white marking with jagged sides.

Vincent used the toe of his shoe and the wine to wash the top layer of dirt off the tile to see if there were any other markings on that particular tile. “What is it?”

Father Chance poured the rest of the wine on the floor in the surrounding area of the exposed tile and revealed another dark blue tile, painted just like the one they uncovered first, only a couple of feet away.

Hope couldn’t take her eyes off the one with the white-painted center of the tile and had an idea. “It's a star. The tiles in the floor represent the Heavens.”

Michael agreed with Hope’s evaluation. “On Earth as it is in Heaven. This floor could be a Space-scape. A depiction of the Heavens at a certain time of year.”

They all took a good look around at the floor and realized that, over the years, the once beautiful mosaic tile floor had been covered with a layer of ground-in dirt that was hiding the tile’s true and meaningful design.

Father Chance assessed what they were all thinking. “We're gonna need a lot of hot water but first we’re going to need to move all the pews back.”

While Michael and Vincent started to work as a team, they moved the pews off to the side, as Hope took Father Chance off to the side.

In a low whisper, Hope asked, "Do you really think there could be a treasure hidden somewhere within the monastery?"

"I think this whole building is a treasure. Have you ever noticed anything special about the three stained-glass windows that are on the West wall?"

Hope took a glance over her shoulder at the artwork behind the altar. "No. I just figured their value was in their design and what they depicted. Why?"

"I only noticed it myself a few years ago. The lead that holds the pieces of glass in place is not lead at all. It's pure silver. And in the center display, that's not brass."

Hope tried to take a better look from where she was standing but it was too hard to tell for sure. "Are you telling me that the glass in that window is being held in by gold?"

"Like I said, I believe this whole monastery is a treasure one way or another."

"So, you think it's true?"

Just then Michael walked over to where Hope and Father Chance were having what they thought was a private conversation.

Michael leaned in and tried to speak in a low whisper. "You know, you can't get away with a whisper in a church, especially with the acoustics of this one."

Hope gave him a wry smile. "So, you heard?"

From across the room, Vincent answered, "Yes, we heard."

CHAPTER 18

All of the church pews and furniture in the monastery had been pushed aside to make room for the four of them to clean the floor as best they could.

Vincent used a small hand truck to wheel in a standard-size oak wine barrel which was about half filled with hot water. He and Michael tipped it over enough to splash out about half of the water onto the floor. Father Chance and Hope each had a stiff push broom and began to scrub away the grime that had camouflaged the details in the flooring. On the other side of the room, Hope used a small pale to scoop out some more water from the barrel to rinse away the debris they had worked loose. Vincent used her broom to continue to loosen up the dirt as Hope kept adding hot water to see how far the mosaic had stretched across the floor. As it turned out, the patterns seemed to take up about three-quarters across the width of the floor and from the bottom step of the altar, led almost out the front door.

It had taken a while, but after filling the barrel half a dozen times, their hard work paid off and what was exposed left them all astonished at what they had revealed.

Michael wrung out the hand towel and draped it over the edge of the opening of the wine barrel. Father Chance came from the back area with fresh clean towels for everyone to clean up their face and hands with. Hope watched as Vincent used a towel under his foot to grind away the last of the smudge exposing another star on a blue tile. Dirty water had built up near the front door so Michael used one of the brooms to sweep it out onto the porch before it could leak back in and spoil their hard work. Father Chance was holding open the front door allowing Vincent to splash out the last of the water from the barrel as a final rinse as Michael pushed the excess grime off the porch and down the steps.

Hope squeezed out a wet towel into a bucket and used the dampened cloth to clean away and expose what seemed to be the last blue tile. She looked around and saw a pattern the tiles had created in this section of the floor where she was standing.

They all gathered and took in the full image that was created on the floor. It was a night sky with four distinct patterns of stars, a crescent moon, and a swirling Milky Way made from smaller broken tiles weaving its way across the sky.

Hope was in awe, “It's amazing. All this time, Father, you never knew this mosaic was a part of the floor?”

Michael saw something else. “It reminds me of that painting by Van Gogh.”

Father Chance saw it, too. “Yes, it does, but this one has something more.” He turned and closed the front door and locked it. “This monastery has been here for over one hundred years. I've only been here for a little more than twenty of those years.”

Vincent set his broom aside and took in what they had exposed. “So, what does this mean? This is a clue, right?”

Michael pointed out different patterns on the floor as he walked around the room. “Look here, here, and over there. These look like constellations.”

Vincent used his finger to draw the patterns he saw in front of him as the others caught on to Michael's discovery.

Father Chance nodded in agreement. “He's right. The word, Mazzaroth, is a biblical Hebrew word found in the book of Job that has more than one meaning. Its literal meaning is, a Garland of Crowns, but its context is that of astronomy and it is often interpreted as a term for the Zodiac, or in this case, the constellations.”

Father Chance and Michael walked over and took another look at the Christ figure that was hanging on the cross. Hope was curious as to what they were looking for and joined them.

Hope went on to explain to Vincent what he had missed out on earlier. “A garland can be a wreath of flowers worn on the head or in this case…thorns.”

Michael finished the thought. “And a king wore a crown.”

Both Father Chance and Michael took a good look at the crown of thorns that was worn by the Christ figure. They then looked at each other and then to Hope. She smiled, thinking the same thing.

Vincent walked up behind them. “What is it? What do you see?”

Hope understood, as well as Father Chance and Michael, that they didn't want to give Vincent another reason to betray them. “It may be nothing. Let's try to figure out the constellations.”

Michael turned away from the group and started to concentrate on the constellation that was closest to him. “Does anyone recognize any particular patterns that are laid out here?”

Hope had turned the other way and looked at the pattern she was standing next to and pointed out its design. “I think these here, they form a triangle with two legs, might represent Libra.”

Father Chance stepped back and watched as Hope worked her way around the room to do her best to make out the groupings.

Michael opened an app on his cell phone, made a few swipes, and then matched up what he saw with one of the patterns on the floor. “It looks like these four tiles next to me represent Aries.” He swiped across his phone again and pointed at the two blue tiles near one another at Vincent’s feet. “Vincent, where you're standing, those two tiles look to be one end of the sign for Taurus, the bull.”

Hope moved over closer to the main doors and pointed out the last of the four constellations. “That just leaves this one.”

Vincent joined her to get a better look. He looked at Michael and asked, "Are there any of them V-shaped?" Vincent made a hand gesture pointing out his observation.

Michael walked over to where they were standing to get a better idea of which set of stars to compare it to. "That could be Pisces."

Hope looked all around the room and then in the direction of Father Chance. "But which ones are we meant to focus on or to follow?"

Michael and Vincent followed Hope's plea and turned to Father Chance for the answer.

"I was assigned to this monastery to protect its secrets. How would it look if I betrayed that trust?"

Hope needed to know. "Does that mean you know which one is the right one to lead us to the crown?"

Michael and Father Chance caught on to what she had just revealed, and they all hoped that Vincent hadn't caught the fact that she had just confirmed what they all suspected, that the crown was real, and it was located here in the monastery.

Michael tried to cover and was quickly back on his phone and reading aloud more of the info about each of the other signs of the horoscope. "It says here, as the final sign, Pisces has absorbed every lesson, the joys and the pain, and the hopes and the fears learned by all of the other signs."

Vincent concluded as the rest of them did, "I guess we're going with Pisces."

Michael took a closer look at the pattern on the floor that represented Pisces. Something wasn't right. He walked the V-shaped pattern and stopped where it veered off. "It looks incomplete." He continued to follow the pattern to where the missing star should be. It led him to a pedestal with an urn sitting on top of it that was filled with holy water. They just assumed it had been placed there for parishioners to dip their fingers in, to then form the cross as they entered the church. This action of touching your fingers to your forehead, which represented the mind, then your shoulders and your heart with the sacrament. This was performed in faith, and it was to impart grace to the believer.

"There should be another star that appears to be hidden under the base of this pedestal." Michael put away his phone and put his hands on the sides of the three-foot-tall, hand-chiseled marble stoup.

Hope reached out to Michael and put her hand on his arm stopping him. “Don't move it. It's not about the missing star, it's about where it is leading us.”

Michael looked in at the still water inside the basin of the stoup.

Hope looked over to Father Chance for some sort of sign and she took his silence to mean she was on the right track. “What do you see, Michael?”

“I see my reflection in the water.”

Hope smiled as she kept her gaze on Father Chance. Hope continued, “Someone once told me you need to look beyond yourself to find true happiness.”

Father Chance couldn't help but smile and Hope returned his faith in her with a smile of her own.

Michael changed his focus from the surface of the water to see a carving in the bottom of the basin. “It's a lion! I see a lion!”

As a group, they took it as a clue and began looking for another lion either carved or that was part of one of the paintings hanging within the monastery.

Hope was feeling anxious, "I don't see any other lion figures."

Vincent got an image in his mind and went with the prospect, "But the lion is the king of the jungle. That's another reference to the king, so I think we're on the right track."

Michael was spinning another theory. "Wait a minute. We've had an earth reference and a water reference. That's two of the four elements. That leaves fire and air. We need to find something that could represent fire and air."

Hope went going back and forth between the two theories. "Then why the lion?" Then, in her mind, she went back to the original Bible reference that started all this. "Michael, what does it say about Leo as a sign?"

Michael reopened the app he had referred to earlier and swiped through a few pages. "This might be it. Leo, as a sign of the Zodiac, tends to be drawn to music."

Father Chance was at the altar in prayer and was holding his rosary beads as he silently passed the beads through his fingers. It just so happened to be the set of rosary beads that were handed down to him by the monsignor who was missing the cross.

When he was done, he stood and faced the others as if one of his prayers had just been answered. "I have to give you all credit. From what I was told, no one has ever gotten this far."

Father Chance thought back to something the monsignor had told him about the monastery and its belongings. He was told never to move anything from where it was, to never sell any of the artwork, and if the day should ever come to pass down the set of rosary beads to the next caretaker with the blessing to never betray the secret of the monastery's true design.

That is what the monsignor was trying to do the day he died. To pass down to Father Chance what his true mission was as the caretaker. To keep everything in place, believe in yourself, and find someone who has the faith to one day, do the same. Preserve the sanctity of the church and all its possessions. Both heavenly and earthly bound.

After the monsignor's passing, Father Chance had painstakingly pieced back together the pieces of what was left of the worn pages of parchment that had been kept hidden in the bookshelf.

Over time, and with many hours of research from the rest of the books in the monastery's library, as well as the library downtown, he was able to decipher the history of the building. Who designed it and why it was set in this particular location?

Even where the monsignor was buried was a predestined act. Even the headstone had been carved with everything but the date of his death. Taking care of this monastery was literally this man's life work and when he picked Father Chance to take over upon his death, he felt that too had been preordained. Father Timothy Murphy was born in the Napa Valley, was an only child, and knew when it was his time to go, he needed to find a man whom he knew he could trust to carry on the promise to only pass the monastery and the land it sat on to someone of true faith.

CHAPTER 19

Hope, Vincent, and Michael gave Father Chance their full attention.

"As I said before, when I took over as curator to watch over this monastery, I was asked to protect its earthly treasures. As of today, I truly believe there is an actual treasure of some kind. One beyond the art, statues, and stained glass."

"Why is that father?" Hope replied.

"I knew about the mosaic floor but not about the constellations. You've been able to find patterns involving elemental references in them, not only physically but also metaphorically." Father Chance held out his set of rosary beads. "I was given this rosary when the monsignor passed away not too long after I arrived here. I was asked to keep them in my possession at all times."

Michael noticed there was something different about them and walked up to get a better look. "Has the cross always been missing?"

"Yes."

Hope tried not only to reassure herself but Father Chance as well. "Father, we are not asking you to break your vow to help us."

"Hope, what you don't understand is, if there truly is a treasure, we just might need it to save this place. I have also taken a vow to only give this place over to someone who has proven their faith." Conflicted, he looked around and weighed what was in his heart against what his head was telling him to do. "You see, this land was set aside for one hundred years and could not be sold. That time has nearly passed. If we do not find this treasure, there may not be a monastery to protect."

Hope did her best to protect the faith she had in herself as well as Father Chance. "Then we'll just have to find it."

"Does this mean you're going to help us?" Vincent asked.

"If it means saving the monastery and the land that it sits on, yes."

Vincent followed up. "Does that mean you know what the reference to the lion is?"

"I think you guys are on the right track with the idea of the four elements." Father Chance walked over next to a statue of a Cherub playing a flute along the North wall. "Wind." He pointed at the instrument. "It takes wind to play the flute in order to make the music."

Vincent and Hope were curious and joined Father Chance at the base of the statue to see what they could make of the possibility of the wind reference.

Michael stayed back in the middle of the room and put himself in between the statue of the Cherub where he thought the flute might be pointing and began looking in that direction. It seemed to be pointing right where he was standing. He thought he saw something across the room and went to take a closer look. "If wind is the key, and the flute is the clue, the flute seems to be pointing…right…here." He took another quick look around and saw nothing out of the ordinary. "Am I missing something?"

Father Chance knew it wasn't going to be left to happenstance and someone stumbling onto a location to offer up a possible insight. "Second Samuel, twenty-two eleven says, He mounted the cherub and flew; he soared on the wings of the wind."

Hope had thought of another possible reference. "The Book of Job." She snapped her fingers a few times trying to help her find the reference. "The east wind carries him off, and he is gone; it sweeps him out of his place."

Father Chance confirmed the passage. "Job, twenty-seven twenty-one. I'm glad you paid attention in class."

The cherub statue at present was facing West and the flute was pointing South toward the center of the room.

Hope offered up a suggestion. "And in order for his wings to ride on the East wind, we need to turn the statue out of place."

The statue was quite tall and must have weighed hundreds of pounds. It was going to take all four of them to turn the statue upon its pedestal until the wings were facing East. On their first try, it didn't budge. Over the years, the statue seemed to have settled firmly in place.

Vincent stepped back and made a suggestion. "How about we try rocking it?"

Father Chance quickly replied, "How about we don't."

Hope asked, "Is there a way we can pry it loose from the floor?"

Michael turned and saw the hand truck that had been set aside over by the pews. He retrieved it and slid the flat edge up under the rounded bottom edge of the base of the statue.

The other three each took a side as Michael braced the wheels with his foot and used the leverage of the dolly to try to lift one side of the statue. It started to lift but it also started to bend the lip of the dolly. He lowered it back down. "Well, it's loose. But still too heavy."

Hope looked across the room and saw the set of candles known as the rack of votives. They were used by parishioners to light when saying prayers. Next to the candles was a small urn that had a small metal bowl on the top of it, filled with sand to put out the used long stick matches.

Hope crossed the room and returned with the bowl of sand. "I only need you to lift it just enough for me to toss some of this sand under it."

After doing this process three times on different sides of the statue, Hope set the sand aside. "Now let's try turning it."

Once again, they each took a side, got a good grip, and pushed. The statue moved.

They were a bit surprised, but least of all, Hope.

Father Chance pointed, in his best estimation, East. "Okay. Let's take this in small increments. No one needs to get hurt."

After a few timely pushes and resetting their feet, the Cherub's wings were now perpendicular to East. They all looked at one another when they saw that the way the Cherub's torso and head were turned, the flute was now pointing in the direction of the altar.

Vincent tried to get behind the statue to look straight down the axis of the flute. He wasn't quite tall enough.

Hope stepped in. "Vincent, lift me up."

Michael moved in and helped Vincent to lift Hope up. As she sat between them up on their shoulders, she was high enough to get a better look directly down and along the flute's shaft.

Where it pointed, there was a candle sitting on the center of the back edge of the altar. The three-inch round candle stood eight inches tall and was set within a four-inch circle. The four-inch circle itself was inset one inch into the back of the shelf of the altar.

Father Chance went to the altar and lifted the candle from the circle and showed it to Hope. As he turned away from the altar, Michael noticed the indented four-inch circle slowly rose and became flush with the back of the altar.

From where he was, he could barely make out a design in the middle of the pad. It looked to be an old worn-out symbol of a fish.

Michael tried not to make it obvious and took a quick look. He noticed there were two more four-inch circles on the back of the altar, one located at each end. On the left corner, there was a brass vessel holding communion wafers and on the other end, a goblet of wine. Michael did not let on to what he had discovered and joined the others.

Father Chance held out the candle for everyone to see. “As far as I know, this candle has been a centerpiece on this altar for as long as I have been here.”

“Why was it never used?” Michael asked.

“I was told it was one-of-a-kind and it belonged to one of the first monks to watch over the monastery, so out of respect, no one has ever used it.”

Father Chance set the candle down next to the medallion in the center of the altar.

Hope was trying to keep everything straight in her head. “Of the four elements, fire is the only one we haven't found.”

Vincent suggested, "Maybe it's time we light the candle?"

Father Chance knew right where to go. "Corinthians. Their work will be shown for what it is because the day will bring it to light. It will be revealed with fire, and the fire will test the quality of each person's work."

Vincent sounded confident. "Hello. If that doesn't say, light the candle, I don't know what more you need."

Father Chance moved over to a side table with a three-pronged Candelabra on it, opened a small drawer, and removed a box of matches. He returned to the center of the altar, struck the match, and with a little hesitation, lit the candle.

Vincent was all out of ideas. "Now what?"

Hope replied, "Maybe it needs to be replaced to where it was?"

Wanting to hide his previous discovery, Michael stepped in. "I'll do it."

Michael moved in next to Father Chance and used their bodies as a shield to block the view from Hope and Vincent.

He took the candle and gently set it back in place in the center circle. As he did, the circle dropped an inch from the weight of the candle.

Father Chance noticed and gave a glance to Michael but said nothing.

Everyone stepped back from the altar to get a better perspective.

Hope couldn't get something off her mind and had to ask. “Father, why didn't you tell us about the lease coming to an end, until now?”

“I figured if it happened, it was God's will, and I'm ready to move on. The monastery has no successor in line to take over the custodial duties. This place is going to take a lot of work to restore it to what it was meant to be.” Father Chance gestured modestly and then much more broadly. “All of this used to be one of the finest vineyards in all the valley. Time has taken its toll, and a lot of equipment needs to be updated. That costs money. There are other vineyards ready to take over this land, knock down this old relic of a monastery, and expand their vineyards. They have the means and soon will have the opportunity to do so. I did not want to put that burden on you and Vincent.”

Father Chance put his arms around Hope and together they took a good hard look at the beauty that was invested in the art within the monastery.

The candle on the altar began to fizzle like a Roman candle on the 4th of July. Sparks began to flicker from the wick. The flame began to get larger and more luminous. Suddenly, the flame grew even brighter then burned out. What was left of the wick fell inside leaving a space within the shaft of the candle.

Michael lifted the candle from its circle and did his best not to reveal the circle itself coming flush once more with the back of the altar. He turned and presented the candle to Father Chance who in turn took it and peered down inside the melted opening. The candle's soft center had melted away leaving access to the space inside. There appeared to be the tip of an object wedged inside.

Father Chance used both hands to grip the inside of the candle, and using his thumbs, he pulled at the rim of the candle and opened it up more to reveal the top of a shiny object that was hidden inside. "There appears to be something down inside the candle."

Hope couldn't stand it. "What is it, Father?"

Father Chance dug in with his fingers and could feel the object. He turned the candle to get a better grip and dug a little deeper. “Whatever it is, it's stuck in there pretty good.”

Vincent pulled out a knife from his pocket and opened the larger of the two blades. Father Chance set the candle on the edge of the altar and Vincent began to slice into the side of it about halfway down. He turned the candle ninety degrees and made another slice.

Father Chance gripped the rim of the candle and was able to open it up enough to get access to the center of the molten candle. He reached in and pulled out a chunk of wax revealing the object. He worked the object loose and was able to remove it.

Hope was mystified but had a good idea of what she was looking at. “Is that…”

Father Chance knew what it was too. “A crucifix. Yes, it is.”

From the very beginning, the four original monks knew they had to do something to preserve the history of the monastery. That included leaving clues to pass on to each monsignor who would take over as keeper of the flame. The flame being, the sanctity of the church and knowing one day the secret it was holding would be its salvation.

Each monk had designed a specific key to each of the steps that would one day reveal the location of the treasure. It was Father Daniel who was taught by his father and his father before him to not only become a skilled carpenter but also a craftsman with the patience to work very intricate and elaborate details into small wooden toys for the children of the family. It was he who removed the cross from the rosary he was wearing and after hand carving a set of specific dimensions into it, he then hid it within the candle to hopefully, one day, be found when needed.

That rosary was then to be passed down to every man of faith who took on the burden of caring for the monastery. The meaning of the word monastery itself gave weight to the task at hand. It is from the Greek and means to live alone.

CHAPTER 20

Father Chance removed as much of the loose wax as he could from the crucifix that had been hidden inside the candle and revealed it was approximately two and a quarter inches in length, was rectangular, and made from pure silver.

Hope noticed the silver link was still attached to the cross and was similar in fashion to the links of the set of his rosary beads. “That looks like it could be the missing cross from your rosary.”

He picked up his rosary and compared the links to the one still connected to the cross. “I believe you're right, Hope.” He could tell right away the design matched the beads. “It is the missing piece. I’m sure of it.”

Father Chance grabbed one of the candles from the three-pronged Candelabra. “Hope, grab that box of matches and light one of these candles for me.” Hope did as she was asked. Father Chance then waved the crucifix just over the tip of the flame to help soften and melt away the rest of the wax still clinging to the cross. Most of the wax came off but left a few little bits still molded near the end.

Hope had noticed how the wax had, in a way, preserved the cross. “It's beautiful.”

Father Chance agreed. “Yes, it is.” He took a good look at it from all sides. He saw there was a small plug of wax stuck in the bottom of the cross and some more wax pressed into the back of it. “Interesting.”

“What is it?” Michael inquired.

“There appears to be some writing on the back of the cross.”

Father Chance gripped the cross by the smaller end above the piece that formed the horizontal part of the cross and waved the longer end back and forth over the lit flame of the candle to melt off more of the wax. After about 10 seconds, he tapped the cross on the edge of the altar to release the softened wax to expose the small grooves, which were etched in the back of the cross. He pointed out what appeared to be three words. “What do we have here?”

Vincent was just as curious as everybody else. “What does it say?”

Father Chance gave Hope a good look at it. “That lettering is much too small for me. Hope you've got better eyes than I do. Can you make out what it says?”

Hope leaned in, "It looks like it says, Day of Salvation."

Father Chance was reminded of the reference. "That's also a reference from Corinthians but I'm not exactly sure of the entire verse."

While Father Chance was trying to recall the passage, he slipped the crucifix into his pocket as he looked around the inside of the monastery and found himself focused on the grandfather clock standing in the corner of the room, off to the right side of the altar.

Hope, in the meantime, had gone to the altar and was flipping through the Bible that was laid open. She stopped when she found what she was looking for in Corinthians. "Here, Second Corinthians." She scanned her finger over the verse. "In the time of my favor I heard you, and then the day of salvation I helped you. I tell you, now is the time of God's favor, now is the day of salvation." She put her fingertip under one of the words. "Salvation is mentioned twice."

But Michael had also noticed something. "So is the word, time."

Vincent noticed that Father Chance had not taken his eyes off the antique grandfather clock. “I'm guessing time is the clue and that grandfather clock just might be part of the answer.”

Hope confirmed it was an antique. “That clock hasn't worked for as long as I can remember. It's older than me.”

Father Chance agreed, “It's older than all of you combined.”

The seven-foot grandfather clock was made of Redwood. The exterior glass protecting the case was so old, that one could see ripples and waves of the cylinder glass it was made from. The pendulum was hanging still behind the three cylindrical counterweights that were each eight inches in length.

The artistry of the clock was masterful. Another creation of Father Daniel’s along with the help of Father Richard and Father Gregory. The numbers one through twelve were hand-carved into the circular twelve-inch face. Just above the six was a small five-eighth-inch hole. The artwork in the lower half of the face was a depiction of what appeared to be stars dancing on the surface of a pond and the upper half was of rolling hills with trees.

The crown of the clock, as well as the base, were exquisitely handcrafted making this clock truly one-of-a-kind.

Hope made a conclusion that seemed to fit her working theory. “Like everything else in here, it must be here for a reason. We just have to find out what it is.”

Vincent grabbed onto the small silver knob that gave access to the tall portion of the cabinet holding the weights. “I think it hasn't been used in so long, the door is jammed shut.”

Father Chance put his hand over Vincent’s to keep him from pulling the knob off. “Hold on.”

Father Chance moved around to the side of the clock and ran his hand down the long axis of the back side of the clock. He felt his fingertips run across a piece of folded metal that turned out to be a small lever. He slipped the lever between two of his fingers and slid his hand down. The action released a latch and the long door on the front of the clock popped open.

Vincent was as surprised as Michael and Hope. “How did you know about that?”

“Compared to you guys, I’m old, too.” Father Chance replied.

Vincent carefully opened the door and looked down into the well of the clock where the counterweights end up if you don't reset them in time. He started to reach down into the tight space.

Father Chance suggested, "I'd be careful if I were you."

Vincent rethought his strategy and instead, grabbed one of the counterweight chains and started to give it a slight pull.

Father Chance cautioned Vincent. "Wait. You're supposed to use your other hand to help lift the weight to keep the tension correct. At the same time, be careful not to lift the weight off the hook from which it hangs."

With one hand he cautiously pulled the corresponding chain, giving it some tension, and with the other hand lifted the cylinder until he was able to raise the counterweight about eighty percent of the way up the center of the clock. "Well, that one seems to be working."

Michael made a request. "Vincent, try resetting the other two and then the pendulum."

One at a time, Vincent was able to lift all three cylinders enough to see if the mechanisms inside the clock's gearbox were still in working condition.

Once he had all the weights in position, he reached behind the chains and with a slight nudge, hand-started the pendulum. After a moment, the pendulum lost its momentum and came to a stop on its own.

Michael had a thought, "Maybe it's locked or something and needs to be reset?" Michael pointed at the small hole just above the six. "Father Chance, is there a key anywhere for this clock?"

Vincent started to feel around in the bottom of the well as Hope looked all around the sides of the clock and reached up and ran her hand across the top. "Nothing."

"What's the key going to look like?" Vincent asked.

Michael held the candle Hope had lit and used the light to see if he could see deeper inside the small hole that was just above the six. "It's going to be about two inches long and about a quarter of an inch round with a hole in the end of it."

Hope stepped back away from the clock. "All I could find was the lever Father Chance used to open the case."

Vincent cleared back out of the way as well. "I got nothing."

Father Chance felt inside his pocket and removed the missing cross from his rosary. He looked at the square base of the cross and saw a plug of wax still lodged in the bottom of it. He took the lit candle from Michael and made his way back over to the altar. He put the base of his cross just above the flame. The wax started to soften and a moment later, he tapped the base of the cross on the edge of the altar. He turned the cross upside down and saw where the wax had once been plugged, was a one-eighth inch square hole up inside the shaft of the cross. He ran the open end of the cross over the flame once again to make sure all the wax was out.

Father Chance returned to the clock and showed Michael what he had found. "Something like this?"

Michael took the small crucifix and inserted the end of the cross into the hole above the six. It fits perfectly. "Here goes nothing." Michael gripped the cross where the vertical crossed the horizontal and slowly turned the crucifix, acting as a key, a quarter turn to the right.

There was a loud CLICK!

"Now what" Vincent asked.

Father Chance responded, "Be patient."

A moment later, the first of the three counterweights began to slowly drop. It stopped after dropping about a foot. So far, the mechanisms that Father Gregory had designed with his blacksmithing skills were still in working order.

Michael turned the key another quarter turn. Click! The second counterweight began to slowly drop, and it too, stopped after moving approximately twelve inches. Michael's hand was getting sweaty, and his heart was racing as he slowly turned the key another quarter turn. There was a longer pause than last time. They could see the weight was trying to drop but it was having trouble. Over time dust had gummed up the works a bit and eventually gravity won. The weight dropped into position and was followed by another…Click! The third weight had come to rest even with the other two.

There was a long pause, and everyone seemed to be holding their breath. That was followed by a whole lot of nothing. Where there once was excitement, there was now just disappointment. Then another, but subtle, CLICK!

A secret drawer that was hidden in the base opened slightly. The drawer was rectangular, ten inches across and three inches high.

It was Father Daniel's intricate design that had blended the face of the drawer with the facade of the base of the clock that had kept the drawer well hidden.

Vincent knelt in front of the clock and slowly guided the drawer open the rest of the way to reveal a bed of spider webs covering something. He carefully peeled back one corner of the web and revealed a dead scorpion.

Vincent quickly jumped back at the sight of the once poisonous predatory arachnid just in case it was still alive.

Hope knew of her brother's phobia for spiders and, although they both knew it was dead, with a bit of dry sarcasm, she asked, "Are you alright?"

Father Chance was quick to remind him, "I told you to be careful."

Vincent gathered himself and asked Michael if he could borrow his knife. He used the tip of one of the blades to tap on the dead husk of the scorpion to make sure it was truly dead. Using the blade from the knife, he peeled back the cotton candy-like webbing to reveal a crown of thorns, made of gold. Vincent was in awe and spoke under his breath in a whisper to himself, "Bingo."

There in front of him was a crown made of pure gold. It was almost a perfect replica of the one on the head of the Christ figure behind the altar.

The thorny crown of Father Richard's design was elongated and about seven to eight inches wide at its widest apex. Being a consummate metallurgist, he was able to weave the four strands of thinly crafted vines together with open spacing between each one to give it volume. The vines themselves contained forty thorns among them to give reference to the forty days and nights of a period of preparation and trial or a new beginning or an event in salvation history. What came to mind as Father Richard was making the crown was the forty days and nights Christ fasted in the wilderness before starting his public ministry. The thorns were each about three-quarters to an inch long and were sporadically intertwined throughout the crown.

Father Richard taking on the task of making the crown of thorns from pure gold was going to take all the skills he had learned over the years from other master craftsmen. From an early age, he knew what he wanted to be. An artist. As a young man, he had visited one museum after another learning to appreciate the works of art that were now considered priceless.

That became his goal as well; to make something that no one had ever seen before, and once they did, they would never be able to stop thinking about it.

The Christ figure that hung above the altar was stored in what the monks referred to as the vault. There was no lock, only a space where the completed designs and products with clues for the ones of true faith, to follow, and achieve their quest.

Father Richard was able to take plenty of measurements off the actual crown from the life-sized Christ figure.

The monks had agreed Father Richard was the man, and they would do whatever they could to help him complete the obligation of making the best representation of the crown as he could with what he had, and what he had, was gold.

It took all four monks doing the mining themselves, to keep the location of the mine secret, over two months to collect enough gold for Father Richard's masterpiece. First, he had to make a mold of a single strand of a vine with ten thorns, which he would repeat the process four times. That process included melting the gold, pouring it into the mold, and then painstakingly cleaning up the rough edges of each vine and thorn.

When Father Richard was ready, he had each monk take a vine, hold it over the flame to soften it up, and they weaved the four vines together. It took a series of heating, bending, shaping, and cooling down periods to complete the entire process.

Once it was done, Father Richard spent hours filing, sanding, and polishing the one-of-a-kind treasure that the crown became.

When the golden crown was completed, Father Richard felt as if he knew why he was meant to be on this Earth and to be one of the four men tasked to use their collective skills to create such an alliance.

CHAPTER 21

Vincent removed the treasure that was made from solid gold and brushed his hand across the crown to clean off a few of the remaining spider webs. He pricked a finger on one of the golden thorns. For a moment, reality hit him. As he saw a trickle of his blood running down the thorn, it gave him an eerie feeling of what the entire crown would look like with Christ's blood on every thorn.

He shook the thought from his mind and stood up to show the rest of them what the monks deemed so precious that they went to all trouble to hide it, and for good reason. "Can you believe this?" It was as if Vincent's feet did not even touch the mosaic floor as he crossed the room over to the basin of holy water that stood next to the front door. He dipped the crown in the Holy water disregarding its sanctity and gently swished it around to rinse away the webs and the spot where he left a touch of his own blood. He let the crown lie in the water as he removed his shirt. He lifted the treasured crown out of the basin, shook off as much of the water as possible and wrapped it in his shirt to dry it off the best he could.

Vincent unwrapped the crown and was completely mesmerized and he spoke as if he was the only person in the room. "Would you look at that?" He lifted the Golden Crown of thorns over his head then turned to face the others. "Can you imagine…" He snapped out of his gaze and asked the others, "What do you think it's worth?"

Father Chance, Hope, and Michael all looked at one another and had a sense of uneasiness that overwhelmed them. Their gut feeling was justified as Vincent began to walk backward toward the front door that was only a few steps away. "I'm sorry to hear about your lease, Father." His words were chilling. "But I have debts to pay too and if I don't cover them soon, I too will be crucified."

Vincent opened the slide bolt on the inside of the door and pulled it completely out. Before Hope could cross the room, Vincent had opened the door, stepped out, and slammed the door shut behind him. He quickly shoved the bolt through the outside handles.

When Hope reached the doors, it was too late. From the inside she could hear Vincent sliding the bolt through the outer handles, temporarily locking all of them inside the monastery.

Hope leaned her forehead up against the inside of the massive door feeling such disappointment in her brother. She knew this day might come but she did not expect the feeling coming over her would run so deep. Giving herself a moment to try to understand, she knew it was not her place to feel hate toward her brother for what he had done, so she gently breathed in and out a few times and tried to let what she was feeling subside.

Hope gathered herself and headed back toward the front of the church where she saw Father Chance and Michael facing the altar. "I don't think a prayer is going to bring him back this time. He's taken the crown and maybe the only chance to save the monastery."

Father Chance turned back to face Hope. "There is more to this than that crown."

"What do you mean?" Hope asked as she made her way back to the altar.

Michael picked up the medallion and showed it to Hope. "Do you think they would have made a medallion such as this and not have it be a part of something much bigger?"

Michael stepped aside to allow Hope to see what he was about to do. He reached to the back of the altar and pressed down on the middle four-inch circle. They all watched as he pushed the top of a cylinder down a couple of inches into the framework of the altar. "The clock is not the end of the puzzle, but I think only the beginning."

Father Chance added, "Vincent only saw what he wanted to see and didn't look beyond his own needs."

Hope's curiosity was piqued. "What's with the circle? Did you know about it all along? Why didn't you say something?" After hearing her own words to that last question, she kind of knew the answer.

Father Chance filled Hope in on their discovery. "Michael noticed when we lifted the candle, the circular platform the candle was resting on lifted as well. Like it was maybe connected to a counterweight of some kind."

He moved to the left and removed the communion vessel. When he did, the four-inch platform that it was resting on rose slightly to become flush with the back of the altar.

Michael moved over to the other end of the altar on the right and removed the goblet of wine from the circular platform there. Again, they all watched as the platform came up flush with the back of the altar.

"How does the medallion tie into all of this?" Hope asked.

At that moment, Father Chance was in the dark as much as she was. "I don't know. We'll have to find out the meaning of the medallion and its other functions together."

He laid the medallion down in the center of the altar. All three of them took a good hard look at it to try to find a clue from its design to form an opinion of what other functions it could possibly have.

Michael started running through his thoughts aloud. "Why three pieces? Why is one gold, silver, or copper? What are the functions of the stones? Why…"

Hope interjected, "Why are there twelve stones?" She reached out and touched a few of the stones that were inlaid in each of the three pieces. "Do you think the stones have something specifically to do with it?"

Father Chance was thinking the same thing. “Yes, I'm certain they do.” He continued, “Why these stones?

Hope pointed to the center of the medallion where all three sections came together. “The center hole is square, about the same size as the base of the cross. Do you think the cross is to be inserted into the medallion?”

Michael went over to the grandfather clock and removed the crucifix from the slot where the cross had been functioning as a key. Father Chance and Hope brought the medallion over to where Michael was standing in front of the grandfather clock. Michael tried to insert the end of the cross into the square hole in the center of the medallion. It didn't fit.

Father Chance went back to what the passage had said, “Maybe, now is the time of God's favor, refers to how time is expressed on the clock?”

Michael saw Father Chance’s gaze locked on the center of the clock face. “What is it, Father?”

"There's something about this clockface that isn't quite right but I can't put my finger on it." Father Chance reached up and opened the smaller glass door that protected the face of the clock. He had noticed the peg that held the hands in place was also square. He pressed his fingertip on the end of the peg, drew his hand back, and looked at his fingertip. There was now an impression of a square embedded in his finger. He carefully worked the outer minute hand loose and removed it, and then took the same care to remove the hour hand, and then handed them both to Hope. Father Chance reached back toward Michael, and Michael understood what he was reaching for, and handed him the medallion. Father Chance aligned the hole in the center of the medallion with the peg in the center of the clock. With a little effort, it fit, and he slid the medallion onto the peg the rest of the way.

Michael expressed his concerns. "There are four sides to a square so there are four possibilities of how it should fit onto the peg. If the stones are part of the answer, there could be hundreds of combinations. This could take all day."

“This vineyard was named Golden Dominion for a reason. It is for the way the sun sets on the summer solstice between two mountains on the West side of the valley. On that day, the last of the sun’s rays paint a golden veil over this particular part of the valley like no other.”

Hope was a bit awe-struck at the revelation. “I didn’t know that. How come you never told me that story?”

“I think you were away at school when I learned of it and after that, it never really crossed my mind until now, because now, it makes sense.” Father Chance pointed to the medallion. “Michael, try removing the medallion and turn it so the gold piece is at the top. Like a golden sunset.”

Michael reset the piece. “In that case, these stones seem to align better with the corresponding numbers on the clockface.”

“I think you're onto something, Michael.” Father Chance went back over to the altar and began thumbing through the pages of the Bible. He paused on a verse that could be a clue. “Psalms twenty-five, five. Give me in your truth and teach me, for you are the God my Savior, and my hope is in you all day long.”

“What does that have to do with the stones?” Michael asked.

Hope nodded her head and caught on to what Father Chance had found in the book of Psalms. “My birthday is in January and my stone is garnet. I think each of these are a birthstone and each one of them has a special meaning of their own.”

Michael pulled out his cell phone and looked up each birthstone and their meaning. “Yes, here it is. January is the garnet meaning protection. February is that amethyst meaning wisdom. March is aquamarine meaning serenity. April’s stone, the diamond, means strength. May is hope. June is love. July is vitality. August is beauty. September, the sapphire, represents truth. October is…”

Father Chance interrupts Michael’s findings. “That's it. You said truth, and which one did you say represented…hope?”

Michael scrolled back through the phone. “May. The emerald represents hope.”

Hope was putting the tip of her thumb to her fingertips as she counted off the months. “May is the fifth month and September is the ninth. So, we have five and nine.”

Father Chance was running the verse of Psalms twenty-five, five, once again in his head. “Both truth and hope are mentioned in the verse. It says, guide me in your truth. Nine comes first.”

Michael wasn't sure and had to ask, “Which stone is the sapphire?”

Hope pointed out the blue stone that at the moment was in the one o'clock position. “That one.”

Michael turned to Father Chance and Hope for advice. “Which way do I turn it?”

Father Chance suggested, “The sun rises in the East. Try turning it to the left.”

Michael had visions of being a thief breaking into someone’s safe in the middle of the night. His heart was racing, and he could feel the adrenaline flowing through him with anticipation. He got a firm grip on the medallion and carefully turned it like a dial to the left until the sapphire lined up at nine o'clock. The room was so quiet you could hear the CLICK echo inside the church.

After turning the medallion, the emerald now sat at about two o'clock. Michael pointed to the green stone. “This is the emerald, right?”

Hope replied, "Yes. That looks like an emerald."

Father Chance suggested, "Now try turning it back to the right, toward the sunset, until you align the emerald with the five."

Michael turned the medallion back to the right until the emerald lined up at five o'clock. The CLICK was just as loud as the last one but this time it came with a quick rubbing sound of metal across wood and ended with a knock. "That did something."

The silence was broken when the grandfather clock let out one loud thunderous chime. BONG!

Everyone stood back waiting to see what would happen next. As the sound of the time faded, they all stood there in dead silence waiting for another hidden drawer to open or a shift of some other kind, but nothing happened.

"What are we missing?" Michael asked. Getting no response, he began to look around the room and went over all the steps they'd gone through thus far. "The constellations led us to the lion. The lion led us to the flute. The flute to the candle…"

"You left out a step. The beginning, as in…" Father Chance pointed to the ceiling and then to the floor. "God created the heavens and the earth."

As Hope was listening to Father Chance, she was facing the grandfather clock at that moment and was studying the design that had been hand-carved into its face. "On Earth as it is in Heaven."

Michael may have been too close to see what she was looking at, so he moved in behind Hope to get a look over her shoulder to see her point of view.

"All this time," Hope said with a sense of awe.

Michael at first couldn't see what she had honed in on. From over her shoulder, he scanned the entire face of the clock for a clue of what she had discovered. Above the outer rim of the numbers was a smaller matching arch that sat within the larger arch that formed the top of the clock's bonnet. In that window was where the moon dial normally would rotate, but on this clock, there was a sun. The sun had a cross in the center of it. Below that, none of the numbers seemed to have anything different about them.

He squinted and cocked his head trying to see from another perspective, like it was one of those sets of two pictures that had minor differences and the challenge was to find the mistakes. He still couldn't see it. "I give up."

"Don't ever give up, Michael." Father Chance replied. "Like God's forgiveness, all you have to do is ask."

"Okay, Hope. What am I missing?"

"The carved numbers appear to be on a separate outer circular track from the center image of the Eden and sky carvings."

"Okay, I see it. What am I still missing?"

"The Eden motif is on top, and the stars are on the bottom. Heaven and Earth are opposite of where they should be."

Michael stepped out from behind Hope and reached out toward the face of the clock as if being drawn into a trance. In his mind, he already saw the reversal of the image and of course, it made perfect sense. Hope stepped out of the way to allow Michael to get a straight-on view of the clockface and a better look at the carvings.

Michael used both hands by putting his left hand over the Eden design and his right over the stars on the bottom half of the wheel. Cautiously, he tried to turn it to the left, but it wouldn't move so he reversed his hands and tried turning to the right. Still nothing. Michael stepped back. "What do you think it is?"

Hope suggested, "Remember the slide after the click. Maybe a lock was moved out of place. Try pressing the center of the face in and then turning it."

Michael reset his hands and gently pressed on the inner circle. From behind, Michael felt the resistance from a spring of some kind and did not release the tension as he slowly tried to turn the dial to the left. It was moving.

All Father Chance could say was, "On Earth as it is in Heaven."

Michael finished reversing the images so that Eden, the representation of Earth, was now on the bottom and the sky was above. He let up on the pressure and felt the inner clockface reset flush with the numbers.

CLICK!

They could all hear sets of small gears rotating within the upper cabinet of the grandfather clock. Then a moment of silence was followed by another loud chime that rang out, filling the confines of the empty church with a resounding BONG!

CHAPTER 22

Michael stepped back as the echo of the grandfather clock's loud chime dissipated throughout the monastery. What followed was a lengthy spell of silence before Michael asked, "Now what?"

Hope noticed the pendulum was still. "Try swinging the pendulum again."

Michael reached in and gave the pendulum a light push to get it started. They watched as it eventually slowed once more to a stop.

Hope figured the pendulum had to come into play somehow. She thought about how most of the clues led to something about the object being designed to have more than one purpose. She stepped forward and suggested, "How about this?" She reached in and gripped the pendulum's shaft and gave it a slight downward tug.

There was a solid CLICK followed by the sound of a metal spring lever uncoiling, eventually leading to another Click.

Hope stepped back and joined Father Chance and Michael as they watched all three counterweights, one at a time, unwind with a slight resistance from the gears. Each weight lowered itself into the well of the clock and came to rest on the bottom as each chain was now at its limit of how far it could go.

Michael stepped in a little closer and propped open the long glass door on the front of the clock so he could see down inside where the weights had loosely collected. He reached in and picked up the first weight that had already slipped off the hook that had suspended it on its chain.

The cylinder was a little heavier than he thought it would be. He assumed it was filled with sand that had given its heft. After giving it the once over, Michael handed over the brass-plated counterweight to Father Chance. He looked it over thoroughly. Upon turning it over, he found what appeared to be a maker's mark punch into the base in the shape of a dove.

Hope asked Michael, "Can you hand me one of the weights?"

Michael unhooked the second weight from its chain and handed it to Hope.

Hope measured the probable weight of the cylinder in her right hand with a slight up-and-down motion. “Father, hand me the other weight.”

Father Chance put the weight he was holding in Hope’s left hand to compare. “I think the first wait is a little heavier.”

“They usually are. Each weight has a different function within the clock. I believe the one on the right powers the chimes which strike on the quarter hour. The middle one serves the pendulum, leaving the left one to power the heavier strikes on the hour.” Father Chance reached out and took the second weight from Hope. He looked at the bottom of it and saw a different maker’s mark punched into it of a cross. “Michael, take a look at the bottom of the third weight.”

Michael grabbed the third weight that was still resting at the bottom of the clock, and he unhooked the chain.

To satisfy Father Chance’s request and curiosity, Michael turned over the cylinder, and there, stamped on the bottom of the weight, was a symbol of a cross.

They were each now holding a separate weight upside down so they could see all three marks that were stamped into the bottom of each cylinder. Hope and Michael switched weights to check both the difference in weight, but also to get a better look and the maker's marks.

Hope surmised all three symbols. "We have a fish, a bird, and a cross. Could the bird be a dove?"

Father Chance gave his interpretation of the symbols. "What we have are the symbols for the Holy Trinity. The cross for God, the fish for Christ, and the dove for the Holy Spirit."

Hope responded with, "The Father, Son, and the Holy Spirit."

Michael asked. "Father, what did you do with the hands you removed from the clockface?"

"I have them," Hope replied. She reached into her pocket, removed the dials, and handed them to Michael. He then removed the medallion from the center post and handed it to Father Chance. He reset the longer of the two dials and began to turn the minute hand around the face of the clock. He kept an eye on the circles. As the cross in the arched picture window rotated to the right, a circle with a fish rotated in from the left.

Michael pointed to the cylinder Father Chance was holding. "Let me see the mark on your cylinder." Father Chance angled the bottom of the brass tube so Michael could see the impression that had been hand-tooled into the bottom. Michael, in his mind, cross-referenced the images on the clock he had just seen with the worn image of a fish on the four-inch pad when he removed the candle from the back of the altar. "I think I know where these are supposed to go."

Michael took the weight with the cross symbol on it from Hope over to the altar and set it on the far-left circular pad on the back of the altar. "The Father."

The four-inch circle slowly dropped the cylinder down into the altar about six inches. The muffled sound of mechanical gears and levers could be heard within the altar.

Father Chance set the one he was holding with the fish symbol and placed it on the middle circle. "The Son."

The four-inch pad dropped down into the altar about the same six inches as the first one, then stopped. Another set of mechanisms grinding within the altar, followed by a metal-on-metal click.

Hope took the last cylinder with the dove on it and approached the altar. She set the counterweight on the pad on the far right. “And the Holy Ghost.”

At first, the four-inch circular platform only dropped about an inch before coming to a stop. Hope stepped back from the altar. “Why isn't it dropping?”

Michael stepped up and took a closer look. He removed the weight and noticed some wine stains on the four-inch pad. “I think that over the years enough wine may have been spilled on the pad to cause it to stick. Michael set the counterweight back on the pad, and like before, it only dropped about an inch.

Father Chance went over to the same drawer where he had the matches. “I have something I think that can help us out.” He removed a small glass bottle and presented it to Hope and Michael. This is the Oil of Catechumens. This is the oil I use during baptisms. It is normally used to strengthen the ones being baptized to turn away from evil, temptation, and sin.”

Father Chance handed the bottle over to Michael, “I guess in this case, oil is oil.”

Michael set the last cylinder aside and poured a little bit of the oil around the outer edges where the pad made contact with the drop shaft. He pressed down on the pad a few times while working the oil in. Each time he had done this, the pad only moved about an inch or two. Now that the oil had lubricated the inner rim, he was able to press down the pad and add a little more oil. He waited a bit and dripped in a little more of the sacramental oil and let it set for a minute. Michael reached in to work the pad up and down but this time, the pad gave way and dropped even further.

As Michael continued working the pad up and down and was about to pour in a little more oil, suddenly, the pad dropped about three inches. "I think that did it."

Michael set the oil aside and placed the third counterweight in the center of the pad and they all watched as it slowly lowered itself further into the back of the altar.

This time when the counterweight was in place, the mechanical sounds were a little bit different than before. The muffled sound of a metal latch could be heard releasing from within the altar. A moment later, another latch, and then another.

The top of the altar popped loose and slightly shifted.

Michael turned to Hope. "Did you see that? The top of the altar moved slightly."

"Yeah, I saw it move," Hope replied.

Father Chance gestured to Michael to go to one end of the altar as he went to the other end. They each gripped the wooden trim that ran along the decorative rim of the top and together they lifted the heavy wooden top of the altar from its base. They all reacted to a musty smell that came out of the base of the altar. When they lifted the top of the altar off, they were careful not to knock over the weights that were still perched on the descending pads. The cylinders themselves were aided by metal rings to hold them in place as they were lowered through the top of the altar. Father Chance and Michael held their breath, and with Hope's help, they set the top on its side and leaned it up against the front of the altar.

Both Father Chance and Michael were at a loss for words as they both just stared into the inside space of the altar. Hope had to see what they were looking at and ran around to the back of the altar so she could get close enough to see inside. She couldn't believe what she was looking at. "Is that-"

"A set of stairs," Michael replied.

Father Chance was just as amazed at what they discovered. "Yes. A set of stairs."

The stairs ran from the right side of the altar down and to the left. There was enough ambient light to see where the stairs ended some fifteen feet below but nothing beyond that. Along with the stairs, was a solid handrail made from a single piece of redwood that ran parallel to the stairs on the left side of the interior wall.

It took their eyes a moment to adjust and to be able to look down into the empty void that was a large, cavernous area below the surface of the church.

More than the emptiness, what caught their eye was the elaborate set of mechanics that were on the West wall of the altar. Da Vinci would have been impressed with the simplicity but creative combination of skills it took to make the locking mechanism.

The preplanning of the stone architecture of Father Sebastian was very impressive. With the added intricacy of Father Gregory's ironwork of hand-made gears based on the inside workings of a clock, the sight was nothing short of amazing.

There was a gathering pallet, a rack and rack hook, various gears, and multiple coil springs, that all functioned based on the varying weights of the grandfather clock.

Michael was curious enough to lift the brass cylinder closest to him, the one with the dove, to see what would happen. When he did, the release of tension slipped a metal pin back into place that would have relatched to the top of the altar to lock it down. He put the weight back on the receptacle pad and they all watched as a tension coil coiled, a metal lever rotated and tripped a spring that drew back the pin meant to hold the top in place.

Without saying a word, they all appreciated the collective effort it took for all four monks to design this altar and to make it last for all this time.

Michael reached in and unlatched three wooden dowels on each side of the end panel that was holding the right side of the altar snuggly in place. He removed the panel which exposed the access to the top of the stairs that led downward into the darkness below.

Father Chance relit all three candles from the Candelabra, handed one to each, Michael and Hope, and kept the last one for himself.

Michael took the lead. He stepped over the four-inch rock base, got his bearings on the top step of the stairs, and began to descend the staircase. With his left hand on the rail and his right hand holding the candle, he made his way down. He used the candle's flame to burn away a few of the cobwebs that were strung across his path.

Hope waited for Michael to make it to the bottom before asking, "Can you make out anything? How big is the space?"

Hope could see Michael move his light from side to side trying to make out the dimensions of the space.

"It's a large shaft. I can't make out how far back it goes. It looks safe enough, come on down and take a look for yourself." Michael replied.

Hope looked over at Father Chance and he made a gesture. "You go on. I'll be right behind you."

Hope found her footing on the top step and then cautiously made her way down into the shadowless subterranean cavern. Once Hope reached the bottom, Michael turned and reached out his hand to help guide her down the last few descending steps.

Father Chance watched from over the rim of the altar as Michael's flame disappeared as he went deeper into the empty void. He could make out Hope's flame as she turned and looked back up at him before facing forward and began to trace Michael's footsteps.

Father Chance came around the front of the altar and as he reached the top of the staircase, he stood there holding out the candle, looking at the mechanisms that lined the inside of the wall of the altar. He could feel his chest tighten and his breathing started to come more quickly as his mind began to play tricks on him.

He knew there were things from his past he would have to face one day and if he stood there long enough, today just might have been that day. He thought, if there was a Hell on Earth, this would be it. His hope for the future of the monastery was brighter than the fear of his past coming to light, so he took a deep breath and gathered his faith. He held the candle out in front of him and entered the descending stairwell.

CHAPTER 23

Along with the ambient light that illuminated the rock staircase coming from the monastery, Father Chance stood about halfway down the steps to get a closer look at the mechanics that had been hidden inside the altar for all these years. The steps themselves were three feet wide and made from perfectly placed flat stones that were a foot deep and had a rise a bit higher than normal of about eight inches. To get the best perspective he could, he leaned back against the redwood handrail that was attached to three pieces of wrought iron that had been mortared into the wall and ran parallel the entire length of the steps.

Ten steps into the tunnel, Michael had his left hand on the wall that ran alongside and parallel to the bottom of the steps, as he held the candle in his right hand. Hope was right behind Michael and had her right hand on his left shoulder with her candle in her other hand, held out to the left. She could barely make out the other side of the tunnel. "This tunnel has to be twenty feet wide." Hope moved her candle side to side and then held it out in front of her to try to see what was ahead of them. "How far do you think it goes?"

"I have no idea." Michael reached up and estimated the ceiling to be about eight feet high. "As bad as the air is, it's really not that bad. We're not that deep underground so there must be some venting built in along the length of the tunnel."

Hope kept her hand on Michael's shoulder to help keep her bearings.

Michael moved his candle closer to the wall to get a better look at the texture. He then turned to Hope, "This is not your ordinary tunnel."

Father Chance was still standing in the middle of the stairwell. He could hear Michael talking to Hope and then his tone changed, "Father, you need to see this!"

As Father Chance descended the rest of the stairs, he lightly ran his hand over the gears and levers appreciating the craftsmanship that went into the design of the mechanics that lined the inside of the back wall of the altar.

Hope met Father Chance at the bottom of the staircase to help guide him to where Michael had made his way about fifty feet into the tunnel.

Father Chance was cautious for two reasons. One, his eyes hadn't fully adjusted, and the other, because he did not like dark, confined spaces. "What have you found? What is this place?"

The walls seemed to be made of a dull white rock. Michael panned his candle over a bit to the left to reveal the wall was lined with slabs of quartz. A small shiny reflection of gold appeared in the quartz. He continued to pan to the left, and as he did, the little flecks of gold became larger ones.

Hope reversed her position with Father Chance so he was now between her and Michael so he could get a better look at what they had discovered. As Hope turned away to head back to the stairs, she got ahead of herself with her enthusiasm. "We're going to need a lot more light."

As Hope quickly moved away from Father Chance, her motion caused his candle to flicker out. Michael could sense a change in Father Chance's demeanor. "Are you okay, Father?"

"I'll be okay."

Michael tried to help Father Chance walk back over toward the steps and to help get him some relief. As he did, he could feel resistance from Father Chance, as if his body was frozen stiff. Michael tried to light Father Chance's candle with his own but when he held out his flame, he felt him flinch.

When he did, he knocked out the flame on Michael's candle. He felt Father Chance had dropped his candle when it landed on Michael's foot. He could sense Father Chance was quickly becoming disoriented. What little ambient light there was coming from the stairwell, was not enough to keep Father Chance from disguising his claustrophobia from Michael any longer.

Michael helped Father Chance lean back against the wall to help him get a sense of where he was in the darkness. Michael remembered his cellphone had a flashlight app. He took out his phone and activated the light function and it immediately illuminated their surroundings. He put his arm around Father Chance's shoulders and tried to reassure him he was going to be okay. "I'm right here with you."

The two men could hear Hope returning as she made her way down the stairwell. "Sorry, it took so long. It took a while to find the extra batteries."

As Hope made her way closer to the men, she noticed Michael was holding his illuminated cell phone in one hand, had his free arm wrapped around Father Chance's shoulders, and both of their candles were extinguished on the floor of the tunnel. "Is everything alright?"

Michael could sense the relief in Father Chance when the tunnel was lit up by the two flashlights Hope was pointing in their direction. Michael felt the tension in Father Chance's body start to release and his breathing started to calm. "We're fine. We just decided to wait for you before we went any further."

Hope handed one of the flashlights to Michael, who promptly handed it to Father Chance to give him a bit more awareness of his surroundings.

Between the direct light from the flashlights and their beams bouncing off the walls that contained quartz and granite, the once dingy and blackened space was now pretty well-lit for the surrounding twenty-five feet, then after that, the strength of the light quickly tapered off.

Hope could see beads of sweat on Father Chance's face. She watched him as he took a deep breath and regained his composure. She sensed something had happened but when she was about to ask, she saw Michael give a little shake of his head as if to say, let it go.

Michael wanted to change the subject, so he had a question for Father Chance. Michael took him by the same hand he was holding his flashlight with and guided the beam to a specific place on the wall just behind him. There on the wall where Father Chance had been leaning was a piece of quartz the size of a basketball. In the center of it was a smattering of dimly faded gold fleck. Father Chance used the material of the black long-sleeved shirt he was wearing to rub the grime away with his elbow. Hope already had her light on the spot when he lowered his arm suddenly, the dull fleck was now bright and shimmering.

Father Chance reached out and ran his fingertips over the little bits of gold that were lodged in little pockets of the larger quartz to make sure what he was seeing with his eyes was not a dream.

Hope lowered her light and Father Chance pointed his light back at the small cluster of gold to make sure it hadn't disappeared. She stepped around Micheal and redirected her light back onto the wall just past Michael. She caught a glimpse of what was to come. As she passed behind Michael, he heard her confidently say, "There's more. A lot more."

Hope slowly made her way deeper into the tunnel. When she returned, she put her arm around Father Chance's shoulders and gave him a one-armed hug. "I want to show you something." Hope kept her arm around him, to help make him feel he was not alone, as she took him deeper into the tunnel.

Father Chance kept his light half pointed down the tunnel and half on the wall. As they walked, the little smattering of gold fleck became a long stretching finger of solid gold. As they traveled deeper, the finger of gold was getting wider, and in some places, began to branch off with each finger getting wider and wider. Before long, the smaller veins of gold were now as large as the top of a small coffee table.

Up ahead about thirty yards, Hope and Father Chance could see Michael shining his light back and forth between both sides of the tunnel. As they caught up to Michael. he was frozen and staring in complete amazement at the wall. He was looking at a deposit of gold the same size as himself as if he were looking in a mirror.

When they caught up to him, he reached out and pushed the light Father Chance was holding toward the wall behind him. There, in the beam of light, was another deposit of gold roughly the same size.

Both Hope and Father Chance turned their lights deeper into the mine. As far as the light could breech the darkness, both sides of the tunnel revealed veins of solid gold as far as the eye could see.

Michael spoke with pretty good assurance he was right. "Father, it looks like the monks knew what they were doing when they built your monastery right over the entrance of a gold mine."

Michael had noticed the walls had been closing in the deeper they went into the mine. He tried to distract Father Chance. "How far do you think it goes?"

There was no answer. Michael caught Hope's attention and nodded his head in the direction of the stairs to alert her that he thought it would be best if they got Farther Chance out of the tunnel.

Once all three were topside, Hope walked with Father Chance over to one of the pews that had been moved up against the wall.

Hope could see that he was still having a hard time reacclimating from being inside the dark tunnel and asked a favor of Michael. "Can you go to the kitchen and get us some water?"

After a few deep breaths and looking around the entirety of the church, it didn't take long for Father Chance to gather himself. "How much do you think is down there?"

Michael returned with a bottle of cold water that he had already removed the cap from and handed it to Father Chance. "Here you go, Father."

Father Chance took a sip followed by another deep breath. "Thank you, Michael." Followed by a heartfelt, "For everything." He turned back toward Hope. "So, how far do you think the mine goes?"

"I think it goes far enough that you're not going to lose the monastery or the land it sits on."

Micheal gave his opinion as well. "Plus, I think you'll have enough to be able to restore the vineyard to full working order, and then some."

Both Michael and Hope saw a big relief come over Father Chance. Michael could see that he was still a bit overwhelmed by everything that had just happened.

Father Chance gestured and asked Michael to take a seat next to him. "I need to ask a favor of you Michael."

"Anything, Father," Michael replied.

*****

After having already locked the right-side end cap of the altar in place and getting the redwood top back on, Hope was standing behind the altar and one at a time, she lifted the cylinders from their respective slots. With their hands still holding the top in place, Michael and Father Chance could feel the vibration from the metal pins from within, locking the redwood surface down.

Father Chance made a request. "Hope, can you reset those weights back in the clock so I can have a minute with Michael?"

"Of course."

"Also, make sure you remove the crucifix key."

Before he could walk away, Father Chance leaned in and whispered something to her. She nodded and took the weights over to the clock.

As Hope was kneeling in front of the clock reattaching the weights to their respective chains, she could make out what Father Chance was requesting of Michael. The two men began to walk across the newly discovered heavenly scene that was displayed on the tiles leading toward the front of the church.

"Michael, I'd like you to think about taking over as curator of the monastery."

Michael was caught off guard. "How could I? I'm not a monk or a priest of any kind."

"There's no set rule the curator must be either one. It just must be someone willing to have faith and to believe in the greater good."

"Wow. That's a lot to think about. I wouldn't know where to begin."

"Sure, you do. You've been running things for a while now. What you need, is to have as much faith in yourself as I do, or I wouldn't have asked."

Can I ask why you want to leave?"

"It's my time to move on. I need to see the world from another perspective."

"Can I have some time to think about it?"

"Take all the time you need but first, we need to get out of here. I need some fresh air."

Father Chance and Michael were inside the monastery standing at the main doors that were still closed and locked from the outside. Michael took his time and let himself absorb everything he could about what had transpired during the day. He looked at the fresco on the ceiling, the altar, and the grandfather clock, and let his eyes take in the vision of what the four original monks had in mind when they built this monastery. What he hadn't noticed was that Hope was no longer in the church.

"I've been thinking about your offer, Father. I'll do it if Hope will run the business with me. I believe with her help; we can make it work."

"Do what you believe. Because if you do what someone else believes, and you fail, you've got nothing. If you do what you believe, and you fail, you still have hope."

Michael couldn't hold back a slight grin. "Are you saying?..."

Before Father Chance could respond, the bolt that was holding the doors closed from the outside, could be heard sliding across the outer handles. The doors to the monastery then swung open.

There, standing on the landing was Hope. "I heard your offer and I accept."

Hope handed Father Chance the crucifix. "Thank you, Hope." He immediately reattached it to the set of rosary beads he was wearing.

Michael looked at Father Chance who responded nonchalantly, "I sent her down through the wine cellar."

All Michael could do was smile. "I hope I can do Golden Dominion justice. Who knows, maybe one day we will name a wine after you."

Father Chance assured him, "I believe in you. Now is the time to believe in yourself and where your life's journey can take you."

"Where will your journey be taking you, Father?"

"There's a small little vineyard up North in Oregon that was just purchased by a couple of newlyweds that has sent me a letter asking me to come and bless the land to give them a good harvest and make a fresh start. I think I'm going to take them up on their invitation and just see what happens after that."

"We'll miss you around here," Michael said.

Hope stepped in and gave Father Chance a big hug. "Yes, we will. You will always be in our thoughts and prayers, Father. And I mean that in every sense of the word…Father."

Michael suggested something they could all agree on. "How about we share a glass of wine to celebrate?"

Father Chance was willing and able. "I know just the vintage. A 2017 Cabernet Sauvignon." He turned and headed back through the monastery toward the wine cellar.

Hope felt right at home talking to Michael. "I want to thank you for everything you've done to help save the monastery and the Golden Dominion label."

"I should be the one thanking you."

"Why's that?"

"For risking your life to save mine."

"I'd do it again, in a heartbeat."

Michael leaned in and kissed Hope. "Thank you."

"You're welcome."

Hope took Michael by the hand and together they walked over to the end of the porch and took a seat just as Father Chance emerged from the monastery with a bottle of wine and three Mason jars for glasses. They all took a glass as Father Chance poured. After setting the bottle down, he removed the set of rosary beads he was wearing and slipped them over Hope's head, then made sure the crucifix was adjusted properly. "This is yours now."

The path from the monastery continued down toward the vineyard. The vineyard, although in need of care, still had its best qualities to bear.

CHAPTER 24

Vincent stood in front of Bianca who was seated behind the desk in their home office. "I understand you are now the head of Bellacini." He opened his backpack and removed something wrapped in his shirt. He set it on the desk and revealed the golden crown of thorns. He took a seat in one of the leather-bound chairs opposite the desk. "I know I was in debt to Mr. Bellacini, but this should cover my loan and interest."

At first, Bianca didn't say a word. She did her best to restrain herself and not to show her excitement at the treasure that was within arm's reach. "I am not the one you are indebted to." Bianca stood. "I am not a Bellacini."

Vincent did not understand her meaning.

Bianca knew the meaning of the priceless piece of art and all that it stood for. With that in mind, she made the sign of the cross by touching her forehead, "En el nombre del padre…" She lowered her hand, "y del hijo…" She passed her hand across her chest from left to right, "y del Espiritu Santo." She then slipped out from behind the desk just as Adriana walked into the room with Alejandro.

As Alejandro moved over and stood next to Bianca, he took in the ambiance and grandeur of the office, thinking he had worked at and for Bellacini for over half his life and had never been in this room.

Adriana walked past Vincent and took her rightful seat behind the desk, as the sole living heir to the Bellacini fortune. Bianca was just fine as her daughter had become the face of the company, and in her eyes, she was now the queen of the valley.

Vincent sat down opposite Adriana. "Wow, this is great! You're taking over Bellacini vineyards until your father returns?"

Adriana took a glance over toward her mother. "Oh, I don't believe he's ever coming back. As owner, I now assume all the responsibilities, including all debts."

"So…"

Adriana cut Vincent off. "Before we get down to business, I'd like you to meet someone." She gestured toward Alejandro. "My grandfather, Alejandro."

Vincent stood and shook Alejandro's hand. "I never knew…"

"Neither did I until recently. He will now oversee the day-to-day production here at Bellacini from planting on through to bottling." Andriana felt she and Vincent were, in a sense, kindred spirits, and made him an offer. "As far as your debt goes…" She looked at Vincent and gave him the same wry smile as when she handed him back the silver medallion, "I'll consider your debt cleared…"

Vincent gave Adriana his full attention.

Adriana continued, "If, you decide to stick around…" She ran her hand across her belly indicating what was to come, "I could use the help. I could hire you as our merchandising consultant." Her thoughts lingered. "I'm going to need you to do one thing first."

Vincent caught on to the slight hand gesture of the mother-to-be status that she had made. She hadn't told her mother that she was pregnant and implied that if he stuck around, she was willing to see what the future could bring. He felt he was being given a second chance. He looked over to Bianca and Alejandro to make sure they hadn't caught on to her subtle but unexpected offer. He turned back to Adriana and gave her the most endearing response, knowing everything that it was to imply, "Anything."

* * * * *

A couple of years had passed, and the Golden Dominion's grounds were well manicured, the vines properly trimmed, and the bunches of grapes that were hanging on the vine appeared to have an abundance of liquid gold yet to be bottled. A single bunch of grapes varied with a mix of colors from green, light burgundy, and some already purple all cradled in a couple of large green leaves like a pair of gentle hands caressing them.

A hand reached in a plucked a few of the darker grapes from the bunch. Michael crushed one of the grapes and then tasted it for its sugar content.

"I'm so looking forward to this year's harvest," Michael said confidently to himself.

From behind Michael, Father Chance replied. "The question is, will you be ready?"

"Hello, Father. These next few years will set the table for us. Taking over Ceil Bleu from my father along with the new hybrids we've come up with should make for some really nice varieties."

"How are your parents these days? When was the last time you heard from them?"

"It's been over a year since we got the last set of cuttings from them. Even then, all he said was that he and Mom were taking the time to travel Europe for more varieties and if he found anything promising he'd send them along."

Father Chance put his hand on Micheal's shoulder. "I know how much you wished they were here for you today, but sometimes God has other plans we cannot see."

"I don't know everything that happened, but when he said that the vineyard had taken a lot out of him over the years and that he and mom just needed some time to themselves, it came across as something more. I guess one day he'll tell me."

"I'm sure they are praying for you to be successful, and he wouldn't have sold you Ceil Bleu if he didn't think you could handle it." Father Chance reassured Micheal, "Just remember, every day is a day to live your best life. Are you ready?"

Micheal replied with a wry smile, "I'm ready, Father."

The bell at the top of the monastery rang out for the first time in many years. Michael was standing back, away from the crowd that had gathered, standing room only, on the front porch. He was well-groomed and wearing a tux.

Father Chance put his hand on Michael's shoulder. "I think it's time, don't you?"

"Father, I wanted to thank you for coming back to do this for us."

"You know I wouldn't have missed this for the world."

"Oh, and I also wanted to thank you for the baptismal services for Adriana and Bianca."

"I hadn't done one in such a long time, and to be blessed with two of them was a joy. Please tell them once again, it was my pleasure."

Father Chance and Michael made their way up the stairs to the main entrance. Michael paused long enough to wipe off the dust from his rented black leather shoes and to give Father Chance time to walk across the freshly buffed tile floor that shined like the night sky.

As Father Chance approached the altar, there were two large men on either side of the altar dressed in black robes who were keeping an eye on the crowd that had gathered.

When Father Chance reached the altar, he picked up the Bible they had used to discover the clues that led them to this time in their lives.

The Bible had been sitting on top of a clear bulletproof Plexiglas case. As he turned to face the friends and family who had gathered, he revealed the golden crown sealed inside the secured box. There was a sign leaning up against the front of the box that read: On loan from the Napa Valley Historical Society."

Father Chance took his place in front of the altar to face the crowd on this special occasion.

After a couple of deep breaths, Michael entered the monastery.

Michael was amazed at the turnout. Almost every pew was full on both sides of the aisle. He took his position as the groom next to the presiding minister, Father Chance. The murmur from the guests changed as Hope entered from the main doorway. Her blonde hair fell to the shoulders of her white dress as the sunlight backlit her silhouette giving her a heavenly aura. Hanging around her neck was the set of rosary beads Father Chance had given to her. The silver cross was front and center.

* * * * *

Once again, the bell in the tower rang out as the overflow of guests were lined up at the entrance to the monastery and down the steps. Michael and Hope exited through the doorway as husband and wife. Popcorn was used instead of rice, and it rained down over them as they made their way through the guests lined along the way.

* * * * *

A cork from a bottle of Champagne was released and all the guests cheered. Michael poured two glasses and handed one to his new bride, Hope.

"I couldn't have done it without you," Michael said with a gleam in his eye.

"What, gotten married? I hope not." Hope replied.

"You know what I'm talking about." Michael gestured widely. "All this. I can't believe we were able to get as far as we have in just two years."

"You know I've always had faith in you. That's why I agreed to be your partner in all this…and this." Hope kissed Michael and another cheer went up from the crowd that had gathered. A local mariachi band started to play, and the guests began to mingle.

A pop from a cork being drawn from a Champagne bottle shot across the table and landed near Adriana who grabbed it and handed it to her eighteen-month-old daughter, Angelica, who promptly started to gnaw on it.

Bianca, who also had a child in her lap, quickly took the cork from her granddaughter. Her son, Oscar, who was only four months older than Angelica, tried to reach over and take the cork from his mother. She promptly tossed it into Vincent's plate, and he replaced it with a slice of bread dipped in olive oil for Bianca. He tossed the cork back in the direction from which it came.

The cork landed on a table set up with a variety of wines. A bottle of Sauvignon Blanc labeled: HOPE, was set down next to a bottle of Zinfandel that was already opened and labeled: FAITH. Next to it, a nice rich Pinot Noir labeled: CHANCE.

It wasn't long before each of the guests who had all gathered had a glass of wine in hand and were raising it in honor of Michal and Hope.

It was the day of the summer solstice and the sun had made its way to the valley between the West hills and it laid down its golden fleece over the vineyard. Propane gas lanterns stood between the tables giving off some ambient light as dusk was looming on this late June evening.

The tops of the rows and rows of mature vines that made up the vineyard had a warm summerset glow over them as if God was looking down over all of those in His Golden Dominion.

Printed in Great Britain
by Amazon

35015041R00169